NATURAL FAMILY DISASTERS

Five Shape-Shifter Short Stories

JAE

ISBN (print): 978-3-95533-107-8
ISBN (mobi): 978-3-95533-072-9
ISBN (epub): 978-3-95533-073-6
ISBN (pdf): 978-3-95533-074-3

Published by Ylva Publishing, legal entity of Ylva Verlag, e.Kfr.

Ylva Verlag, e.Kfr.
Am Kirschgarten 2
65830 Kriftel
Germany
http://www.ylva-publishing.com

First Print Edition: August 2013

Credits
Edited by Peggy Adams
Cover Design and Formatting by Streetlight Graphics

Table of Contents

Acknowledgments v

Author's Note vii

Bonding Time 1

Coming to Dinner 7

Babysitter Material 51

When the Cat's Away 61

Plus One 73

About Jae 105

Excerpt from Second Nature 107

Other Books from Ylva Publishing 113

Coming from Ylva Publishing in fall and winter 2013 123

Acknowledgments

A big thank-you goes to all the people who helped me write, revise, and improve these short stories: Alison Grey, RJ Nolan, Erin Saluta, Peggy Adams, Astrid Ohletz, Marion Pönisch, and Pam Salerno.

Author's Note

The two main characters of this anthology, Jorie Price and Griffin Westmore, first met in my novel *Second Nature*. The events in *Second Nature* took them on a wild chase from a tiny town in Michigan's Upper Peninsula to an off-the-books poker game in Detroit and then into the council chamber of the most powerful shape-shifters in Boise, Idaho.

Running for their lives didn't leave Jorie and Griffin much time to enjoy their families' company or to share romantic moments. This anthology will give them a chance to do all of that. I hope you enjoy sharing some peaceful times with Jorie and Griffin too.

Jae

P.S. In this anthology, the term "pasties" doesn't refer to the adhesive patches covering a woman's nipples, worn usually by erotic dancers. In Michigan's Upper Peninsula, where these stories take place, "pasties" are meat-and-vegetable-filled pastries.

Bonding Time

GRIFFIN SLID HER FINGERS OVER warm curves and closed her eyes in pleasure. "Mmm." She purred at the return pressure against her thigh.

The unwelcome ringing of the phone interrupted the tender moment.

"I'm sorry." Griffin took one of her hands away and received a disappointed glance. She leaned back against the bed and lifted the receiver to her ear, planning on quickly getting rid of the caller. "Westmore."

"Hey, sis. It's Leigh," her half sister said.

"Hi, Leigh." Griffin's attention was already returning to the body that was snuggled against hers. "What can I do for you?" Over the course of the last year, she had learned to be more polite when it came to family interactions, so a "What do you want?" or a "Not now!" was out of the question.

Leigh started to converse about news on their fathers, cousins, and the rest of the pride in true Kasari style. If no one stopped her, she would go on and on for hours until she felt she had thoroughly caught Griffin up on pride business.

"Leigh," Griffin said. "I'm a little busy right now." Her fingertips trailed up a warm belly and received a groan of approval.

"Oh," Leigh said. "I didn't want to interrupt. It's just that Ronnie went with the dads to meet with the leaders of the Hiawatha National Forest pride." Gus had been mentoring Rhonda, preparing her for her role as Leigh's partner and future natak of the pride, just as Brian had been mentoring Leigh. "The dads didn't want to overwhelm them by bringing a fourth person, so I'm a little bored all alone at home."

A year ago, Leigh never would have admitted a weakness like that to her half sister. If she had, Griffin would have snarled in disgust. Back then, it was beyond her understanding how a grown woman could feel bored or lonely just because she was on her own for a day.

Now things were different.

Last month, Jorie had been gone on a book tour to promote her new novel and had then been stuck in Boise for council meetings for two more weeks. By now, most Wrasa had accepted Jorie as a dream seer and would never think of harming her, so Jorie could travel with just one or two bodyguards. Griffin had stayed behind in Osgrove to get some of her own work done and enjoy some time alone.

The problem was she didn't enjoy it anymore. After a week on her own, she found herself driving over for short visits with her family just to stay busy until Jorie returned.

Now it was her turn to entertain her sister. "Why don't you come over for dinner?" She suppressed a sigh. "I can fill you in on my new job as a park ranger in the Ottawa National Forest and the work I'm doing for the council as a maharsi searcher."

"Dinner? I thought I could come over right now," Leigh said. "Ronnie has a box of books she wants Jorie to sign."

Griffin let her hand trail higher, spreading her fingers out over the curve of delicate ribs. Signing books was not what she had planned for Jorie tonight. "No, Leigh. Right now is not a good time. Jorie and I are both busy." Her gentle touch evoked an enthusiastic response. Griffin stifled a groan. "Ow, sweetie, not quite so hard, please," she murmured with one hand covering the receiver.

"Not a good time?" Leigh asked. "Why not?"

Griffin leaned forward and pressed a kiss to a soft forehead. "Well, right now, we're having a little bonding time."

"Oh," Leigh said. She was silent for a moment and then repeated, "Oh. I'm sorry for interrupting. Please say hi to Jorie for me. Talk to you later. Much later. Bye." Abruptly, Leigh ended the call.

Griffin stared at the phone and shrugged. She looked down at the warm body snuggled against hers. "Just you and me again," she said, knowing that the object of her attention didn't like sharing her affection.

The bedroom door opened.

Jorie leaned in the doorway and stretched as she always did after hours of being bent over the laptop. The sight of her still made Griffin's heart beat faster. "Hey." Jorie padded over on bare feet.

"Hey." Griffin watched Jorie's every move,

drinking her in. "Finished with the scene that has been giving you trouble?"

The dark head tilted in a nod. "I finished it earlier and already sent it off to Ally. You can read it later if you want."

Griffin answered with a smile. Jorie's trust, her willingness to share her writing, was a prize she held dear. "I'd love to. So if you already finished the scene, what were you working on? Got started on a new scene already?"

"No. I was writing down a few things for the dream-seeing manual your mother and I are working on. I think it's a really great idea to have something like that. I sure could have used a little more instruction while I was trying to figure out how it works." Jorie rolled her eyes.

"The council really lucked out with you," Griffin said. A wave of tenderness and pride swept over her, and she studied Jorie fondly. "Not only did they get a dream seer who is giving them advice, they also got a writer to write it all down for them, all in one beautiful package."

A seductive smile teased the edges of Jorie's mouth. "So only the council lucked out with me?" The timbre of her voice made Griffin's body vibrate.

Griffin laughed. "No. I'm one lucky cat too," she said, meaning it. "I never thought I'd find a woman who can give me the space I need as half Puwar and the closeness my Kasari side craves."

"That's easy since you give me the same things." Jorie's gaze rested on Griffin, warm like a touch.

Who would have thought? My perfect mate is a human. The Great Hunter really has a weird sense of humor. "And you can even handle my mother and the rest of my family." Griffin purred with satisfaction.

"Apropos mother." Jorie nodded in the direction of the phone. "Was that my mom? Did she call to ask why her allergies always flare up when the in-laws get together?"

Laughter rumbled through Griffin's chest. "No. She's been so accepting of us that I think it's only fair to give her some time before we tell her why one turkey won't be enough when she invites my folks over for Thanksgiving. Leigh called and says hi."

"Ah. So that's who you were talking to."

"That and her." Griffin pointed at the cat on her lap. "I've been trying to teach her to keep her claws to herself when she kneads my leg, but so far, she's not a quick learner. I think we need more bonding time."

Her words stopped Jorie's approach one step from the bed. "Okay. Then I'll go back to my writing. I wouldn't want to interrupt your feline bonding time." She winked at Griffin.

"Oh, no." Griffin reached out one of her long arms, grabbed Jorie's belt loop, and pulled.

Jorie landed on the bed next to her.

The bouncing of the bed annoyed the tri-colored cat on Griffin's lap. Emmy stood, hopped down, and stalked out of the room.

"Ow." Griffin pretended to sulk. "My cuddle buddy left me. Whatever will I do now? I'm a cat. I need affection."

Jorie's T-shirt slid up when she stretched out on the bed and leaned up on her elbow to grin at Griffin. Bare skin peeked out between faded jeans and the edge of the T-shirt.

Instantly, Griffin moved closer, wanting to touch the warm skin.

"Oh, poor cat," Jorie cooed, "all starved for affection. Want me to scratch your belly?" She slid her hand under Griffin's T-shirt and trailed her fingers teasingly up Griffin's belly.

In the past, Griffin would have had a dozen suave comebacks for that question. No one would have been able to talk to her that way without triggering the urge to reassert her feline superiority. Her role had always been that of the seducer, not the seduced. She had directed lovemaking, not trusting her partner enough to let her have complete control over her body and her heart.

Now and with Jorie, everything was different. Griffin stripped off her T-shirt, lay back on the bed, and whispered, "Yes, please."

Jorie moved down and planted a soft kiss over Griffin's navel, making her chuckle, then purr. "Then let's see how quick a learner you are." She stopped Griffin's hands from sliding under her own T-shirt. "Keep your claws to yourself."

With a sound that was half groan, half purr, Griffin laid her hands onto the bed and let Jorie have full control over their bonding time.

###

Coming to Dinner

"A CHRISTMAS DINNER?" BRIAN SET down his glass on the coffee table and licked a drop of milk from his lips. "You know we don't celebrate Christmas, so why would we start now?"

Griffin stared down at him and at Gus, who was leaning back on the couch and hadn't yet offered an opinion. "Because I'm inviting you to celebrate Christmas with Jorie and me."

"Ah." Her father waved a negligent hand. "Christmas is a stupid human tradition. Invite us over some other time."

A flare of anger made Griffin's skin itch. She scratched her forearms. "Jorie is human and she's my mate, so if you want me to be part of the family, you better get used to celebrating this stupid human tradition!"

"Calm down, you two." With a lazy stretch, Gus looked up at Griffin and then glanced at his brother. "What's so bad about Christmas? Spending time with the pride, eating a turkey or two, and solving the mystery of surprise presents—sounds like the perfect feline entertainment to me."

"What's so bad about Christmas?"

Brian grumbled. "Christmas carols blaring everywhere." He covered his sensitive ears to make his point. "Human cubs on a constant sugar rush from eating too many cookies, and humans strolling through the forest in search of the perfect Christmas tree. The pride hasn't had a quiet, uninterrupted run in weeks."

Griffin had to admit that some Christmas traditions were pretty annoying. The lack of privacy in the forest bothered her too. Last night, a family searching for a few fir branches to decorate their home had nearly surprised her as she had been about to shift shape. Still, she was quickly warming up to other Christmas traditions. So far, the mistletoe that Jorie had hung over the doorway was her favorite. *Not that I'd need an excuse to kiss Jorie whenever I want.* Thinking about Jorie made her anger fade away. She directed a calm gaze at her father. "The dinner is important to Jorie and to me, not just because of Christmas. We want to tell Helen, and I want both of you there to support us."

"Tell her what?" Brian sipped his milk again. "That you and Jorie are sharing the same pillow at night?" He smirked.

A frown replaced Griffin's pleading expression, but she knew her father was just having fun teasing her a little. She took her commitment to Jorie too seriously to laugh about his offhand remark, though. "No." She scowled at Brian. "Helen already knows that Jorie and I are a couple. We want to tell Helen who and what I really am."

Milk spattered all over the coffee table. "What?"

"Jorie has lied to her mother about her sexual orientation—or at least not told her the truth—for so long. She doesn't want there to be any more lies between them." Griffin was secretive by nature and her skin prickled with unease at the thought of revealing the Wrasa's secret existence, but she supported Jorie's decision.

Brian brushed drops of milk from his beard. "Don't tell me the council has given you permission to reveal our existence to a human."

They hadn't, of course. The decision to come out to the human public might take the council years, and Jorie didn't want to wait that long. "Since when did you ever wait for the council's permission?" Griffin asked. "It's a family affair, and the council doesn't need to know we told Helen. I trust Helen. She won't betray us."

"How can you know that?" While Brian had come to accept and even like Jorie, his first reaction was still to distrust humans.

"Helen loves Jorie," Griffin said. "She would never do anything to hurt her—and hurting me is hurting Jorie." It was as simple as that.

The "and vice versa" hung unspoken between them. Hurting Jorie by refusing to come to her Christmas dinner would be hurting Griffin too.

"Fine," Brian finally said. "We'll come. Don't let it be said that a human has more sense of family than a Kasari."

The tension fled from Griffin's body. "It's great that you see it that way, because Mother is gonna be there too."

Brian groaned.

"So, Christmas Day, two o'clock—be on time or dinner will get cold." Griffin shot both of them a glance. "And bring your bag with some of the cat allergy stuff, please. Otherwise, poor Helen might not survive having dinner with eight big cats."

Brian folded his muscular arms across his chest in a feline pout. "I told you I don't make house calls for humans."

"She's not just any human," Gus said. "Since Griffin and Jorie are living together, Helen is Griffin's mother-in-law."

The blood rushed from Griffin's face. She blinked. She had never thought about it that way, but Gus was right. Wrasa law considered a couple married as soon as they were living together. *Huh. What do you know—I'm a married woman. I wonder if Jorie knows—or what she'll say when she finds out.*

Twin grins spread over Gus's and Brian's faces. Brian threw his brother an amused glance. "Seems our daughter never thought about that. Maybe you are right, brother. Christmas could be fun. We never had that conversation about marrying into the pride with Jorie. Might be a nice opportunity to talk to her and ask her about her willingness to bear a litter of cubs for the pride."

A deep growl rose up Griffin's chest. "Maybe I'll just tell Jorie that you refused her invitation after all."

"Oh, no, I'll be there," Brian said. "Now you made me curious—and you know you can't keep away a curious cat. Make sure you have enough food. And don't let Jorie anywhere near the kitchen."

"She's not that bad," Griffin said, automatically defending Jorie.

Silence filled the living room, giving Griffin

enough time to remember the last meal Jorie had tried to cook for her. "Okay," she said. "Jorie stays out of the kitchen."

"Christmas dinner?" Helen repeated. "Oh, how wonderful. Of course, I'll be there. It'll be wonderful to see you again. You and Griffin, of course."

Her mother's constant acceptance of her relationship filled Jorie with warmth. She pressed the phone to her ear with a grateful smile. "It won't be just me and Griffin, though." She wanted to give her mother fair warning. Both of them were used to quiet Christmas celebrations. Even before her father had died, it had been just the three of them, not a big family. "We invited Griffin's whole family—her fathers, her mother, her sisters, and their partners. I hope they won't overwhelm you." For her, it had taken some getting used to.

"Oh, the more the merrier." Helen laughed. "It will be wonderful to meet Griffin's family."

Jorie's stomach twitched nervously. *Let's hope you'll still think that when you learn who they really are.*

"Any idea what I could give them for Christmas?" Helen asked. "I don't know Griffin's family, but I don't want to show up empty-handed."

As far as Jorie knew, Wrasa didn't even celebrate Christmas. "Don't worry about it, Mom. Griffin's family isn't big on presents. If we feed them, they'll be happy."

"With so many guests, I could book an earlier flight and help Griffin with the cooking," her mother said.

Jorie hesitated. At times, Griffin could be pretty territorial about the kitchen. *Or maybe it's just me she doesn't want in there.*

"I don't want to intrude," Helen said when Jorie's hesitation continued.

"You're not intruding. I'm sure Griffin would love to have some help. She's planning a big dinner." In fact, their shopping list read like a supply order for an entire army regiment.

"Wonderful." Joy vibrated in Helen's voice. "I'm really looking forward to spending Christmas with you."

Jorie gulped. "Me too, Mom." Her hands shook when she hung up. *God, I hope I made the right decision.*

"Emmy, no! Get down!" In one tigerlike pounce, Griffin crossed the living room—but she was too late.

The Christmas tree, complete with its tri-colored cat ornament, came crashing down.

"Shit." Only Griffin's quick reflexes saved the Christmas balls and glass figures from smashing on the table with its dinnerware. She grabbed the slender tree trunk. Fir needles bit into her hands, making her growl.

Emmy jumped down from the tree and disappeared under the couch.

Hurried steps approached, and Jorie peeked into the room. Her eyes widened when she saw Griffin with her hands wrapped around the Christmas tree, holding it at an angle. "What are you doing with the Christmas tree?"

"Me?" The glowing star on top of the tree

started to pitch to the side, and Griffin quickly reached up and straightened it. "I didn't do anything. Emmy—"

"You're not sharpening your claws on the Christmas tree, are you, liger?" Jorie crossed the living room and bumped Griffin's hip, making the ornaments on the tree rattle.

"No! But unlike me, Emmy never learned to keep her claws to herself."

A playful twinkle entered Jorie's dark eyes. "Since when are you good at keeping your claws to yourself?" She lifted up on her tiptoes. Warm breath brushed over Griffin's lips, and then Jorie kissed her.

The scent of coconut and spring grass replaced the Christmas aromas drifting through the house. Griffin closed her eyes and sank into the kiss. She slid her hands down a warm back.

"Hey!" Jorie caught the tree before it could fall.

"Oops." Griffin grinned and bent to steal another kiss. "Okay, so keeping my claws to myself isn't my strongest point. But at least I didn't try to climb the tree, like Emmy did."

Jorie shook her head and sighed dramatically. "Cats."

Before Griffin could protest, Helen entered, drying her hands on the "kiss the cook" apron she had borrowed from Griffin. "Griffin, I think the turkey could use another—" She stopped when her gaze fell on the tree Jorie was still holding. "Oh. What happened?"

"The cats in this household can't keep their claws to themselves," Jorie said. She straightened the tree and replaced a few ornaments that had fallen off.

Under the pretense of helping her, Griffin pinched one firm ass cheek.

"Ow!" Jorie glared playfully. "See? You're proving me right," she said, just low enough that her mother couldn't understand. More loudly she added, "Emmy tried to climb the tree, and it almost toppled over."

"Oh, gosh." Helen stared at the tree. "Cats and Christmas trees don't mix well, do they?"

Jorie grinned brightly and gave Griffin a sideway glance. "No, they don't."

"It's a really beautiful tree."

It was. Griffin looked at it with satisfaction.

"Oh, yeah, it's the most beautiful tree on the Upper Peninsula—and I would know because Griffin made me look at all of them before she decided on this one," Jorie said with a laugh. She reached for Griffin's hand and kissed the tiny marks where the fir needles had pressed into her skin.

Griffin had never celebrated Christmas before. For her first Christmas with Jorie, not just any tree would do. It had to be the perfect tree with the perfect decoration. Every string of tinsel was exactly in the right place—or at least it had been before Emmy had decided to climb the tree. Now it looked a little worse for wear. *Well, at least my family probably won't notice since they never had a Christmas tree before.*

The doorbell rang.

Griffin and Jorie exchanged a silent glance. "You and your mom go greet my family," Griffin said. "I've got a cat to get out from under the couch."

Helen stayed back but watched with interest as the first guests entered the house.

A blond, slender woman set down the two covered dishes she carried and wrapped her arms around Jorie in a warm greeting. Her taller companion, loaded down with more dishes and a heavy looking bag, kissed Jorie on the cheek.

Tears of joy blurred Helen's vision, and she quickly wiped them away. After decades of worrying about her daughter, it was the best Christmas present Helen could imagine to see Jorie surrounded by people who cared about her and to have Jorie return the warm greetings with obvious affection.

"Mom, this is Griffin's sister Leigh and her partner, Rhonda." Jorie gestured first to the tall woman, then to the blonde with the friendly smile. "Leigh, Ronnie, this is my mother, Helen Price."

Partner. Right. Jorie mentioned that Griffin has a sister who's gay too. Helen shook hands and helped to carry in bowls and dishes.

The door had barely closed behind them when the bell rang again.

"Leigh, can you help Griffin out in the kitchen?" Jorie asked. "And Ronnie, if you want, you have time to look at the latest chapter before dinner. My laptop is in the bedroom. Just be careful not to let the cats escape. My mother is allergic."

As if evoked by that word, Helen's eyes started to water and a tickle began in her nose. She sneezed twice and helplessly shook her head at Jorie's worried glance. The sudden onset of her allergies surprised her. Before, when she had helped Griffin in the kitchen, her eyes had burned and her nose had itched too, but she had blamed it on cutting onions. But this was clearly a reaction to cats. Usually, her cat allergy was a very mild one. Her neighbor's cat evoked nothing more than a light itching, but something about Jorie's cats made her react strongly. *Maybe it's because she has three of them.*

Jorie opened the door to reveal an auburn-haired woman who tugged at the ribbon around the present she held. When she looked up, Helen met observant eyes the same color as Griffin's.

Again, Jorie made introductions—and confirmed that this was indeed Griffin's mother.

Helen watched Nella Westmore greet Jorie—friendly, but not with the same warmth as Rhonda and Leigh. *Is that just how Nella is, or does she have some reservations about Jorie and Griffin's relationship?* Instantly, Helen vowed to show her unconditional acceptance tonight. Maybe she could help Nella come to terms with her daughter's sexual orientation.

Another car rolled up the driveway before Jorie could close the door. Two men got out and fell into step with each other. A woman followed behind them. They, too, carried covered dishes.

Maybe they thought Jorie would be doing the cooking, so they wanted to bring their own food, just in case. Helen chuckled to herself.

The lighter-haired man reached the door first and didn't hesitate to pull Jorie into a warm hug. "Hey there, kitten." He fluffed Jorie's hair in a fatherly way.

Tears filled Helen's eyes again. *Just the allergies.* But truth be told, the tears had nothing to do with cat hairs and everything to do with the man's greeting. Helen's late husband had always greeted their daughter in much the same way. It was bittersweet to see Jorie have that kind of relationship in her life again.

The second man loomed in the doorway for a moment. He silently touched Jorie's shoulder.

"We're not celebrating Christmas in the doorway, are we?" a female voice asked behind the two men. When they stepped aside, a slender blond woman of about Helen's age walked up and hugged Jorie too.

"Guys, this is my mother, Helen Price. Mom, this is Rhonda's mother, Martha. And these two are Brian and Gus, Griffin's fathers." Jorie stopped. She bit her lip as if she had said too much.

Ah. Helen patted Jorie's hand. *So Griffin has two fathers. Oh, well, what's another gay couple in the family? No big deal, right?* Helen shrugged. *They are people like you and me.* She helped putting away the guests' coats and carried food and presents inside, all the while listening to the family members hugging and greeting each other. They all seemed like one big, happy family.

Except for Nella. Griffin's mother didn't seem interested in interacting with the others. Instead of following the other guests into the living room, she lingered in the hall and looked around as if she was trying to find the quickest way out.

How weird. Helen had looked forward to spending Christmas with Jorie and Griffin since she had learned about the dinner, so she couldn't understand Nella's lack of enthusiasm at all. *Where's her Christmas spirit?* "I'm so glad we finally get to meet each other," Helen said.

Nella nodded but said nothing.

"I think the world of your daughter." Maybe that would get her some reaction and reveal how Nella thought about their daughters' relationship. "Griffin is such a lovely girl."

An auburn eyebrow shot up. Nella eyed her skeptically.

Okay. Helen chuckled. *Maybe calling a six-foot-two woman a lovely girl was a bit over-the-top.* "Before she met Griffin, my daughter lived in a world of her own and didn't socialize much. I'm sure if not for Griffin, she'd spend Christmas just with a bunch of cats."

Now a grin spread over Nella's face. "Oh, no, spending Christmas with a bunch of cats...of course we wouldn't want that."

Is she being sarcastic? Helen couldn't figure out any possible double meaning to Nella's words, so she decided that she didn't know Nella well enough to interpret her tone. "Would you like something to drink? Red wine? White?" Maybe a good glass of wine would mellow Nella a little.

"No, thank you," Nella said. "But a glass of milk would be great."

Helen furrowed her brow. *Milk?* "Ah, sure." She led Nella into the kitchen and poured her a glass of milk. "So have you visited before or do you want a tour of the house?"

"I spent some time here when Jorie and I were working on a book together," Nella said.

"Oh. So you're a writer too?" Helen asked.

"Not exactly. I guess you could say I'm an expert on one of the topics Jorie wrote about."

"Ah, kind of like Griffin." If Helen remembered

correctly, Griffin and Jorie had met when Jorie had researched big cats for one of her books. "Isn't it nice that Griffin's job brought the girls together?"

"Oh, yes." Again, a slight smile darted across Nella's face, as if she was secretly amused about something that Helen didn't get.

Her superior demeanor was starting to irritate Helen. *Does she think her daughter is too good for mine? Or that it's just a phase and their relationship won't last?* "You did know that your daughter is gay before she met Jorie, didn't you?"

"Sure," Nella said. "I knew when she was just a cu—just a girl."

"Mom?" Jorie called from the living room. "Where are you? Don't you wanna join us in the living room?"

Helen gave Nella a nod. Her Christmas mission to make sure Nella was supportive of their daughters would have to wait.

"You can show your muzzle now," Nella said. "I know you are there."

Not looking guilty at all to have listened in on her conversation, Gus strolled into the kitchen. "You know she thinks you are a homophobe?"

"What are you talking about, Kasari?" They had only met a handful of times over the past thirty years, but somehow, Nella always felt attacked by Gus, maybe because she didn't understand him and his sense of humor at all.

"You're not exactly spreading Christmas cheer. Helen probably thinks it's because you don't want to spend the holidays with your daughter and her lesbian lover." Gus's green eyes sparkled with amusement.

"I don't want to spend the holidays with the whole pride," Nella said. "It has nothing to do with Griffin and Jorie." This was exactly why she had insisted on raising her daughters alone instead of accepting Brian's offer to move in with him. Too many pride entanglements and too little solitude.

Gus grinned. "Yeah, but then again, Helen doesn't know that you are the only tiger-shifter in the house."

The human's endless questions were beginning to make sense now. *She was trying to find out if I accept Jorie in Griffin's life.* A glimmer of respect started deep within her. Nella had never liked humans—at least not until she had met Jorie—but she understood the need to protect her cubs. *Well, let's hope revealing our existence to her doesn't go horribly wrong. A mother protecting her cub can be a dangerous opponent—even if she doesn't have any claws.*

"Where's Mom?" Jorie craned her neck. Her shape-shifter guests were looking at the Christmas tree, grumbling about the human need to fell a perfectly good tree and drag it inside, but her mother was nowhere to be seen.

"Relax." Griffin trailed her hands over Jorie's shoulders and gently massaged them. "She's probably just in the kitchen, getting something to drink."

Some of the tension dissipated from Jorie's muscles. "I just want today to go well." Introducing the in-laws to each other was nerve-racking enough, but she also worried about how her mother would take the revelation that shape-shifters existed.

"It will." Griffin squeezed her softly. "Just think how poor Rufus must have felt when he introduced his and Ky's parents to each other. A coyote-shifter, a wolf-shifter, a tiger-shifter, and two lion-shifters—compared to that meeting, today should go just fine."

Helen entered the living room. Her eyes shone as she took in the people crowding around the Christmas tree.

For Jorie, having so many people in her house took some getting used to, but Helen had always loved being around people. *She'll fit right in with the Kasari part of Griffin's family. At least I hope so.*

Helen took a seat on the couch and slid to the side to make room for other guests.

Brian and Gus promptly sat next to her. The couch dipped considerably.

Wide-eyed, Helen grabbed for the armrest.

"See? I told you we should have given Jorie a new couch for Christmas," Brian said to his brother. "Her furniture is not fit for us."

"Brian." Gus's voice sounded as if he were speaking to a three-year-old. "You don't give furniture for Christmas. People want to pick their own couch." He sent Helen an apologetic glance. "Our family is not big on Christmas, usually, so you have to excuse Brian."

"Is it time for the presents?" Griffin asked.

Jorie chuckled. *If she were in her cat form, her ears would perk up.* With typical feline curiosity, Griffin had tried to find out what was hiding in the wrapped parcels hidden in Jorie's closet since the beginning of December. She had pawed them and sniffed them until Jorie had threatened to ban her from the bedroom. "After dinner, Griff."

"But the turkey still needs a little time in the oven." Griffin's whiskey-colored eyes gleamed. "Let's open presents now."

Helen reached out and patted Griffin's knee. "Remember when you were a little girl, Jorie? We always opened presents before dinner, so you wouldn't have to wait so long. Maybe we should take pity on the little one too?" She looked up at Griffin with a teasing grin.

Griffin's family members looked a bit startled that Griffin would allow a human to tease her like that, but Griffin just grinned. Sometimes, she seemed more at ease with Helen than with her own mother. "Yes, please."

"We should at least wait for Ky and Rufe," Jorie said. "It seems they are running late."

The doorbell sounded before she had even closed her mouth.

With a satisfied grin, Griffin strode to the door. She returned with Kylin and Rufus.

Helen's eyes widened when she took in Kylin. *Is it her size or that she looks a lot like Griffin?* With whiskey-colored eyes and wind-tumbled red locks, Kylin resembled her fraternal twin, but for Jorie, they had always looked very different. *Kylin looks good, though.* Her cheeks were flushed from the cold and her eyes shone as if she was as eager to open the Christmas presents as her sister was.

Her guests began to unwrap their presents, and Jorie laughed at the items that were piling up on the coffee table. Except for the books from

Rhonda and Leigh, most items weren't exactly traditional Christmas gifts.

Nella smoothed her fingers over the bow on her present before handing it to Jorie. "Here," she said, sounding as if she were holding the most original present in the history of Wrasa.

Laughter shook Jorie when she removed the wrapping paper and saw what it was—a meat mallet.

Brian nudged his brother. "I thought you said no furniture and no kitchen utensils?"

"Yeah, well, apparently no one enlightened Nella about the do's and don'ts of Christmas presents," Gus said.

Nella straightened her broad shoulders and gave him a cool glance. "I'll have you know that meat mallets are a popular Christmas gift. I bet you can't beat that."

Uh-oh. The cats are getting competitive about Christmas gifts.

Brian handed over his present with a flourish.

"Thank you." Jorie opened the present and revealed two pairs of socks. Tiny paw prints dotted the soles.

"Socks?" Gus arched an eyebrow at his brother. "You gave them socks?"

"They're really warm," Brian said.

"They're great," Jorie said. She felt a little the way she did when one of her cats brought home a dead mouse and laid it in front of her with feline pride. She leaned up from her position, sitting cross-legged on the floor, and kissed Brian's bearded cheek.

A satisfied smirk crossed Brian's face. "What did you get them?"

Gus pointed at the gift certificates Griffin was studying. "Massages for Griffin and cooking lessons for Jorie."

The roomful of people erupted into laughter.

Heat flushed Jorie's cheeks.

Behind her, Griffin vibrated with a silent purr at the thought of enjoying a massage.

Helen leaned down and tugged on Jorie's sleeve. "I see they know your little flaws already." She looked up when a small, wrapped box landed on her lap. "For me?" Clearly, she hadn't expected that anyone in Griffin's family would bring a gift for her.

"Just a little something," Gus said.

When Helen opened the present, a stylish silk scarf, with colors that matched Helen's eyes, landed in her hands. "Oh, how pretty. I had heard that men like you have a wonderful sense of fashion, but I always thought that was just a stereotype."

Men like Gus? Jorie frowned. Most cat-shifters were indeed very fashion-conscious, but Helen couldn't know that.

Brian handed Helen a small, round box.

Oh, no. Jorie eyed the box. *He didn't get Mom jewelry just to outdo his brother, did he?*

When Helen tentatively lifted the lid, no silver or gold sparkled in the lights of the Christmas tree. Instead, a piece of chocolate candy lay in the box.

Just one? Jorie grinned. *Oh, how little he knows human women.*

But Brian grinned as if he had given Helen a precious jewel. "Eat it."

Helen hesitated. Her gaze searched out Jorie. "But dinner will be ready soon, and I don't want to spoil my appetite."

"Eat it!" Brian growled.

At Jorie's encouraging nod, Helen put the piece of chocolate into her mouth. She chewed twice. Then her jaw froze. Her eyes watered, and this time, it had nothing to do with her allergies. Her gaze darted around as if in search of a napkin or a garbage can where she could safely spit out the chocolate, but finally, her good manners won out. She swallowed and then sat gasping. Gratefully, she reached for the glass of water that Martha handed her and gulped it down.

What the hell did he give my mother? Jorie glared at Brian.

Griffin settled down on the floor next to Jorie and whispered, "I think he put the Wrasa antihistamine in there. It tastes awful, but it has no side effects. Having dinner with eight big cats shouldn't be a problem now."

Still, Jorie didn't appreciate Brian giving her mother the medicine without her consent. *Well, it's not like he could ask her. And I'll make him apologize later.*

When the last drop of the water was gone, Helen looked up. "Um, delicious. Thank you, Brian."

Sharp teeth glinted for a moment when Brian smiled. "See, Gus? She liked it." He grinned down at Helen. "I'll give you more of them next year."

"Oh. Um." Helen blanched. "That's not necessary."

Poor Mom. Jorie reached up and squeezed her mother's hand. *Welcome to the world of cat-and-mouse games.*

"Here." Griffin set the biggest present in the room down on Jorie's lap.

Jorie looked from the box to the strangely serious Griffin. Shadows swirled through the whiskey-colored eyes. Did she feel guilty about buying a gift despite their agreement? "I thought we said no big presents this year?" Jorie asked. "We're saving up for a vacation on the Bahamas, remember?" Secretly, Jorie planned to make it their honeymoon.

"Yeah, I know, but this is one thing I still owe you," Griffin said.

Holding her breath, Jorie tore off the wrapping paper. She hoped Griffin's present wasn't anywhere near as personal as hers had been. Heat flushed her skin when she remembered the adult-rated story she had written for Griffin. She had promised to read it to Griffin as soon as they were alone in the house again. The big box opened, and Jorie pulled out a new laptop. "Griffin..." Speechless, she smoothed her hands over the shiny surface.

"Your old one has never been quite the same after you...um...accidentally dropped it," Griffin said, her gaze lowered to the floor.

"Hey." Jorie reached for Griffin's hand and pressed a kiss to the palm. Only the two of them knew what had really happened to her laptop—she had hit Griffin over the head with it when Griffin had broken into her bedroom with orders to kill her. But instead of following orders, Griffin had saved Jorie's life and risked her own. Jorie had long since forgiven her, and she didn't want Griffin to feel guilty anymore. "You didn't have to do that. I was the one who dropped the laptop."

"I know I didn't have to do this. But I wanted to." Griffin looked into her eyes as if they were alone in the room.

"I helped pick it out," Leigh said.

"Yeah, while they left me to shop for all the other presents," Rhonda said.

She was the only one in Griffin's family who actually liked shopping. While the crowds and the noise in malls were simply too much for the other cat-shifters, Rhonda stalked the stores like a lioness on the hunt, searching for just the right prey.

"Then thanks to all of you." Jorie put the laptop back into its box. She knew she would get to play with it tomorrow morning while Griffin took Helen out for pasties. The two of them had made it their own personal tradition every time Jorie's mother came to visit.

Helen handed out little presents to Griffin's family.

Jorie received a fist-sized gift. She hefted it in her hand, surprised by its weight. "No socks." She peeked at Griffin, who held a wrapped present that looked like a book.

"You didn't confuse us, did you?" Griffin chuckled. "Jorie's the one who rarely takes her nose out of a book."

"She won't put her nose in this one," Helen said.

With her typical catlike neatness, Griffin slipped her finger under the tape and removed the wrapping paper without tearing or wrinkling.

Jorie was faster. Seconds later, she held a tiger figurine in her hand. The level of detail was amazing, right down to the whiskers and the white dots on the backside of the tiger's ears. It looked amazingly like Nella's cat form. "Beautiful." Jorie trailed her finger over the tiger's stripes.

"For your desk," Helen said. "Maybe it will inspire you to write a sequel."

While Jorie thanked her mother, Griffin had finally folded the wrapping paper and held up her present. "A cookbook. Thank you, Helen."

When Jorie took a closer look, her throat constricted. This wasn't just any cookbook. It had belonged to Helen's mother. When Jorie had been a child, Helen had often tried to lure her into helping in the kitchen by promising that she would one day inherit her grandmother's cookbook. After years of continued disinterest from Jorie, Helen had given up and accepted that Jorie would never like cooking. "Mom..." If Jorie had ever doubted her mother's acceptance of her relationship with Griffin, these doubts were gone now. Words failed her.

"It was my mother's," Helen said quietly.

Griffin's gaze flew up from the cookbook. "Helen..." She cleared her throat. "Are you sure you want me to have it?"

"Yes." Helen's one-word answer said it all.

"Thank you." Griffin leaned over to hug Helen, cradling her with the gentleness she reserved for family.

"Thanks, Mom. This means a lot to both of us." Jorie took a breath and handed her mother an envelope. "And this is from Griffin and me."

With one flick of her finger, Helen opened the envelope. "Airplane tickets?"

"I want you to be able to visit us whenever you feel like it," Jorie said. Time together was the most valuable gift she could give her mother.

In the past, she had hidden from the world, including Helen, here in small-town Michigan, but all of that had changed in the last year. Her heart and her life felt complete now, and she wanted her mother in it.

Helen wrapped one arm around Jorie, the other around Griffin, and pulled both of them into a shared embrace. "Thank you," she said, her voice trembling with emotion.

The timer went off in the kitchen.

They pulled back from their embrace.

"The turkey is ready," Griffin said.

Before Jorie could even twitch, nine hungry Wrasa were on their feet and heading for the kitchen.

Helen stood too and reached for Jorie's hand to help her up from the floor. "Griffin's family is really lovely," she said, one hand pressed to her chest in a gesture of sincerity. She lowered her voice. "But between you and me, their taste in chocolates is a little off."

Helen stared at the table, halfway expecting it to break down under its heavy burden. A giant turkey sat in the middle of the table, surrounded by two hams, roast beef, meatballs, a large dish of lasagna, and two different pasta dishes. Behind them, on the coffee table, mashed potatoes were piled up in two large bowls. Different breads and rolls stood within easy reach of the main table. Steam rose off two casserole dishes of gravy.

Wow. Helen watched the other guests pile food up on their plates. *It seems they all have Griffin's appetite.* She forgot to eat while she watched them interact with each other.

The young man across from her lovingly picked the juiciest pieces of roast beef and placed them on the plate of Griffin's twin sister. Kylin graced him with a soft smile. Next to them, Leigh's girlfriend stole the corn off Leigh's plate and nudged a bite of turkey over in exchange. Helen's gaze wandered to Gus and Brian, then to Jorie and Griffin, who stole a quick kiss before they reached for their forks.

They are just like any other couple. Not that she had thought otherwise, but before seeing Griffin and Jorie together, she'd never had an opportunity to meet gay people. At first, she had been afraid that being gay would make her daughter even more of an outsider, but now she found that the opposite was true. With her black hair and dark eyes, Jorie looked very different from the rest of the blond or red-haired, mainly green-eyed people at the table, but there was a sense of familiarity and of family that included Jorie.

Jorie seemed completely at ease with Griffin's family; she even teased the gruff Brian. Griffin's sisters and their partners treated her like a favorite sister-in-law.

"Mom?" Jorie asked. "Everything okay? You aren't eating."

Brian grinned. "Maybe she's holding out for more of my delicious chocolate."

Just thinking about that piece of candy made Helen's stomach roil. But at least her allergy seemed gone, now that the cats were safely in the bedroom, so she could enjoy her meal. "I'm fine." She poured gravy over the delicious mashed potatoes that Griffin had made. "I'm just not used to so many people at the table."

"Yeah," Nella said. "It can be a bit overwhelming."

It was, but in a very good way. "Oh, no. It's really nice."

"Now here's a woman who knows the value of family." Brian patted her arm. His fingers lingered for a moment. "And mine is a really lovable family."

Is he just being nice, or is he flirting? Helen peeked at Gus, who was talking to Rhonda's mother, oblivious to his partner's straying attention. *Maybe Brian is bisexual. Or is he flirting with me to hide that he's gay?* She still hadn't figured out the relationship between Griffin's fathers when the last crumb of dinner had disappeared before her baffled eyes.

Without being asked to help, Griffin's family began to pile up empty bowls and plates and carried them to the kitchen.

Helen stood to help too.

Next to her, Griffin's brother-in-law snatched a big pot away from his wife, leaving her to carry a few of the glasses to the kitchen.

Oh, what a gentleman. It seemed that all of Brian's daughters had chosen their partners well.

When they stopped in the doorway, she almost collided with the couple.

"I'm very sorry, Mrs. Price," the young man with the earnest brown eyes said. "But Jorie said it's tradition, so would you mind if I kissed my wife?" He pointed at the twig of mistletoe dangling from the ceiling above the door.

Helen laughed. "Oh, no, go right ahead, young man." She respectfully averted her gaze when they kissed. On her way back to the living room to pick up more empty plates, she passed Gus and Brian. She realized they were the only couple who hadn't even touched hands all evening. *Maybe they think I wouldn't like it if they were openly affectionate with each other.* "You know," she said as they stepped out of the living room and paused under the mistletoe, "I really wouldn't mind if you wanted to kiss each other."

Brian's eyes widened. "Kiss each other?" He looked at her as if that were an utterly foreign concept to him.

"Sure." Helen gave him an encouraging smile. "You're under the mistletoe, after all."

Through squinting eyes, Brian stared up at the ceiling. "And because we're standing under a piece of greenery, you want me to kiss him?" He stabbed a finger in Gus's direction.

"It's fine, really," Helen said. "I'm not homophobic."

"Homophobic?" Brian's brows now almost reached his hairline.

Gus laughed. He trailed his hand up his partner's arm and breathed into his ear. "Oh, don't be upset that she found us out, darlin'."

"What?" Brian shoved him away and continued to stare at Helen. "You think I'm gay? You think we are...? Ick!"

"Something wrong?" Jorie asked when she left the kitchen and found them standing in the hall and Gus laughing hysterically.

"Yes! Your mother thinks I'm gay." Brian grumbled.

He's not? Nothing made sense to Helen anymore.

"She thinks **we** are gay," Gus said. "Gay together." He wiggled his brows.

After a few seconds of baffled silence, Jorie started to laugh so loudly that the others came out of the kitchen to see what was going on. "Oh, Mom." Jorie gasped for breath. "Gus and Brian are brothers."

"Brothers?" Helen's gaze darted from the grinning Gus to Brian, who didn't look amused at all. "But you said they're Griffin's fathers, so I thought..." She stopped, completely confused.

"They are." Jorie sighed. "Mom, I think it's time to explain a few things."

The tension in the house rose noticeably.

"Let's go into the living room," Jorie said. "I think you need to sit down for this conversation."

That didn't sound good. Helen's knees trembled as she followed Jorie back into the living room. *Jorie telling you she's gay didn't shock you, so you should be able to take whatever else she has to tell you.*

"What made you think I'm gay?" Brian called after them.

"Later, Dad," Griffin said. "Right now it's not important."

Someone gently pressed Helen down onto the couch.

Jorie settled down next to her and reached for her hands. "Mom..." She cleared her throat. "There's something I wanted to tell you for a while, but I always chickened out." Fear flickered in her daughter's eyes.

An icy ball formed in Helen's stomach. "You aren't sick, are you?"

"No." Jorie patted Helen's hands. "No, Mom. Nothing like that. It's nothing bad, really. It will just be a bit of a shock because I'm sure you aren't expecting it."

The ball of ice transformed into excited butterflies. "You're pregnant!"

"If that's true, then my daughter is even more talented than I thought," Gus said.

Helen looked up at him. *I thought he wasn't Griffin's father after all?*

"What?" Jorie made a sound somewhere between a cough and a giggle. "No, of course not. Aren't you forgetting something?" She gestured between her and Griffin, who was blushing. "Sorry to be so blunt, but there's no sperm involved in this relationship."

Determined not to show how rattled she felt, Helen looked her in the eyes. "There are other ways nowadays, you know?"

Now Jorie was blushing too. "I'm not pregnant, okay?"

"Okay. If it's not that, what do you want to tell me?"

In the sudden silence, Griffin's family exchanged glances, as if deciding who should tell her. Finally, they all looked at Jorie.

Griffin stepped behind Jorie and laid both hands on her shoulders in a gesture of silent support.

"Mom." Jorie took a deep breath. "You read my new novel, right?"

Helen nodded. She hadn't just read it once. She had read it half a dozen times during the last few weeks. "I loved it. It's the best of all of your works."

A blush dusted Jorie's cheeks. "Thank you."

"I mean it. It's fantastic." The most fantastic thing was that Helen could feel the love between the two main characters, and it made her think that Jorie had written a lot of her own experiences and emotions into the story. *In fact, Quinn reminds me of Griffin.*

"Then I'm sure you remember the shape-shifters?" Jorie asked.

"Of course I do." Normally, Helen didn't read a lot of fantasy novels. But Jorie's shape-shifters... "I loved them. They just seemed so real."

All over the living room, the other guests exchanged meaningful glances. It seemed there was a silent communication going on, and only Helen was excluded.

"Mom, I don't know how to tell you this, but..." Jorie's eyes fluttered shut and then opened again. "They are real. These shape-shifters really exist. And Griffin, Brian, Gus, and all the others here, they are shape-shifters."

Silence spread in the living room. Even Brian's grumbling stopped.

Helen laughed. "Isn't she an amazing storyteller?" She gazed at the other guests. "When she was a child, she amazed her father and me with these fantastic stories about her imaginary friends."

"They weren't so imaginary after all, and what I'm saying isn't just a story. You just had dinner with a bunch of cat-shifters."

"And a half wolf, half coyote-shifter," the nice young man said.

Helen stared at them. Surely they were joking? She couldn't figure out why they thought it was funny, but they had to be joking.

"I think she needs to see it," Gus said.

Again, gazes were exchanged all over the

room. This time, everyone ended up looking at Griffin.

"Me?" Griffin touched her own chest. "Are you crazy? You seriously want a ten-foot liger to be the first Wrasa she sees in her animal form?"

Brian stood. "Let me do it. I'm the natak of the Ottawa National Forest pride after all."

What is he talking about? Helen's confusion grew with every word.

"No." Griffin stopped her father from unbuttoning his shirt. "An alpha male out to prove that he's not gay is not the kind of first experience with a shape-shifter that I want Helen to have."

"Maybe Rufus could...?" Jorie said. "He looks a bit like a large dog and is not quite so scary. Sorry, Rufe. No offense."

The brown-haired man shrugged. "No offense taken. But I don't think I should shift around humans." He looked at his wife. "Not right now. I feel a bit out of control today."

Everything felt so surreal. *Why are they discussing this as if they can really turn into animals?* "Jorie, please." Helen squeezed her daughter's hands. "This isn't funny."

Jorie didn't listen. She looked at the friendly blond woman who had been the first guest of the evening. "Ronnie, would you? Compared to the others, you are small and not as threatening."

"Of course." Without hesitation, the young woman stood and started to unbutton her blouse.

"Um, sweetie," her partner said. "I'm very fond of watching you, but humans don't undress in front of each other. Maybe go to the bedroom, okay?"

When the young woman opened the bedroom door, two of Jorie's cats rushed out.

They hissed at the brown-haired man and ignored the other guests before they disappeared under the couch on which Helen sat.

"Oh, no." Helen prepared for sneezes and watery eyes, but nothing happened. *Weird. This whole evening is getting weirder and weirder.*

Muffled groans and grunts came from the bedroom.

When Griffin's sister opened the bedroom door, the blond woman was gone. In her place stood a golden lioness. Her whiskers vibrated as she rubbed her cheek against Griffin's sister.

Darkness threatened at the edges of Helen's vision. She sank back against the couch.

"I can't believe she thought I was gay," was the last thing she heard before she allowed herself to slip into a soothing unconsciousness.

"Griffin, can you please make your cats stop hissing at me?" Rufus asked. "It makes me want to howl and chase them up a tree."

Griffin looked away from Helen's pale face for a moment. "They're Jorie's cats, not mine."

"They smell like you, though. I bet they sleep on your side of the bed. So please, tell them to stop."

He wasn't joking. Waves of agitation hit Griffin's nose. Even Rufus wasn't his usual quiet self today.

Kylin settled down next to him and trailed her fingers over his arm.

"Did you ever try to tell your own cat to stop

doing something she wanted to do?" Griffin asked, nodding at Kylin. She waited until the truth of her words sank in and a slow smile spread over Rufus's face. "I'm not wasting my breath." At least the three felines in the household had learned not to hiss at fellow cats, as big and as human-looking as they might be. Now only poor Rufus was the object of hissing and bristling.

"Hush," Jorie said. "She's coming to." She lifted the cool cloth from her mother's forehead. "Mom?"

Groaning, Helen opened her eyes and sat up. "God, I had the weirdest dream."

Awkward silence answered her.

"It wasn't a dream?" Helen stared at Rhonda. "You really were a...a lion?"

Rhonda settled down on the edge of the couch next to Jorie. Everything about her was gentle and friendly. Nothing screamed predator. "We are what you would call shape-shifters," Rhonda said. "Leigh and her dads and my mother and I, we can shift into something that you humans call a lion."

"Shape-shifters?" Helen repeated as if giving her brain a chance to catch up.

The Wrasa in the room nodded.

Helen rubbed her temples. No doubt they were pounding. "A-and all you lions are gay?"

"Why does she keep thinking that?" Brian asked.

"No, Mom," Jorie said. "Gus and Brian are both considered Griffin's fathers, but not because they're a gay couple. The Kasari—the people who can turn into lions—consider all members of a ruling coalition the fathers of a child, not just the biological father."

"If it helps you deal with the situation, just think of me as their uncle," Gus said kindly.

Still glassy-eyed, Helen looked at Griffin.

Griffin froze. *Oh, please, Great Hunter. Let her accept this. For Jorie's sake.*

"And you?" Helen asked, sounding as if she was afraid of the answer. "Rhonda didn't include you in her list of lions."

"You said you liked the cover of Jorie's novel, right?" Griffin asked.

Helen nodded.

"Good. Because that's a picture of my cat form." Of course, no one outside of this room and the council knew that. The human readers of the novel probably thought it was just a photo of a liger in a zoo.

Helen's already pale face blanched even more. "You want me to believe that you are this giant..." She gesticulated.

"Liger, yes," Griffin said. *Please don't force me to show you. It would be a bit much for one day.*

Helen pressed the balls of her thumbs against her eyes and then peeked out from behind her hands. "Can you give me a moment alone, please?"

The Wrasa moved to the door.

"You too, please," Helen said to Jorie.

The door fell closed behind them, and Griffin immediately wrapped her arms around Jorie, who slumped against her. "She'll be fine with it," she whispered into Jorie's coconut-scented hair. "It just takes some getting used to."

The rest of the family crowded around them, supporting Jorie with reassuring words and soft touches. Moments like this made Griffin glad that she had grown closer to her family in the past year.

Jorie leaned her forehead against Griffin's shoulder. "I hope you're right."

Chaotic thoughts raged through Helen's head, making it pound. Questions repeated themselves over and over, but she didn't find any answers. *I feel like I'm stuck in Jorie's novel. This can't be real. It just can't. What's going on?*

Nothing made sense anymore.

Helen pressed her hands to her face and massaged her pounding temples.

"You know, I wasn't too fond of having a human daughter-in-law at first."

The unexpected voice made Helen jump. She pulled her hands from her face.

Griffin's father—the biological one—stood in front of the couch. "I don't like humans." His thick beard parted in what Helen hoped was a smile. "Present company excluded, of course."

Helen's insides quivered. She sensed something untamed, something potentially dangerous about this man. She wanted to send him away, but now that she was alone with him, she thought it would be better not to anger him. "Of course," she said but watched him cautiously. *Calm down. If he was dangerous, Jorie would never leave you alone with him.*

With unhurried steps, Brian walked over to the table, reached for a leftover shrimp, and dunked it into the cocktail sauce. He ate with the enjoyment of a cat and then directed his gaze back at Helen. "You humans can be the most dangerous and treacherous animals of all."

Anger sparked and chased away the fear. "Excuse me? I have neither claws nor sharp teeth." Helen stretched out her fingers and pulled back her lips. "I don't hide who and what I really am. I don't spring nasty surprises on people on Christmas Day."

"I told them it was a stupid idea to tell you, but despite their sensitive hearing, Wrasa children don't listen to their parents any more than human children do." Brian stepped closer. "Jorie is showing her trust in you by telling you this, and we trust her enough to let her decide for herself. But there are some Wrasa who wouldn't react so tolerantly. Jorie is risking a lot by telling you the truth."

Helen's protective instincts reared up. "You mean she's in danger?" Her gaze flew to the door. *Jorie's alone with eight of these shapeshifters!* She was about to jump up.

Brian sat on the couch next to her, ignoring Helen's flinch. Almost casually, he put a hand on Helen's arm and kept her in her seat. "She's not in danger from any of the Wrasa in this house."

"But you said you don't like humans. How can I trust you to keep my daughter safe?"

"She's Griffin's mate, and that makes her my daughter too." The wild expression in his eyes gentled. "We all love that little human kitten, okay? She's one of us now."

One of us? New panic rose in Helen.

"Oh, Great Hunter, not in the bloodsucking, 'turning you into one of us' way." Brian rolled his eyes. "She married into the pride."

"Married?"

"They live together, so my kind considers them married."

Hm. Helen blinked. She had hoped that Jorie would be getting married for years. A tiny smile crept onto her face. "Maybe you shape-shifters aren't so bad after all."

Brian stretched out his long legs. "Well, our traditions make a lot more sense than stories about a fat man climbing down the chimney with a sack of presents. That's for sure."

Helen ignored the comment and focused on what was important. So many questions were running through her mind. "When Jorie got together with Griffin, did she know who...what Griffin is?"

"She knew."

The thought rattled around in Helen's brain. She shook her head as if that would help her understand. Why would Jorie choose to be in the middle of all this confusion? All this danger? She helplessly spread her hands. "Then why didn't she break it off? Wasn't she scared?" Even with Jorie there to help her understand, Helen was shaking. She could only imagine how scared Jorie must have been if she'd lived through the revelation alone.

"Oh, she was scared all right. And she had every reason to be." Brian stopped, and Helen had a feeling there was more that he wasn't telling her. "But love gives you the courage to face the scary things."

Love. From the beginning, Helen had never doubted that Jorie loved Griffin. And shape-shifter or not, the feelings she saw in Griffin's eyes whenever Griffin looked at Jorie was clearly love too.

"I know you are worried about your cub," Brian said.

An involuntary smile formed on Helen's lips. *Cub.* Somehow, the term was endearing.

"But I promise you that we'll always keep her safe." Brian's eyes held nothing but sincerity. "We're not animals or monsters. We Wrasa are capable of love, friendship, and loyalty the same way you are."

"I'll try to understand," Helen said. At the moment, that was all she could promise.

"Good." Brian picked a bit of lint from his shirt. "Now tell me something..."

Helen suspected what was coming. She secretly rolled her eyes. After the scary revelation, her patience was running thin. "You know, you really have to get over me thinking you were gay. It was an honest mistake after Jorie introduced you and Gus as Griffin's fathers. Stop being so offended. Being gay is not a bad thing, you know?"

Brian flashed a catlike grin. "That's not what I wanted to ask."

"Oh." Helen looked at him but couldn't tell if he was lying or not. Griffin's father was as mysterious as a cat. "Then what did you want to ask?"

Brian watched her with the intensity of a predator. "You read Jorie's novel. What did you think of Quinn's father?"

Awkward silence settled over the kitchen, only interrupted by Jorie's shaky voice. "Maybe

Brian was right," she mumbled, her head burrowed against Griffin's shoulder. "Maybe telling Mom was a bad idea. This is too much for her. She can't deal with it."

Griffin slid her fingers through soft black strands of hair. "Don't underestimate your mother. Give her a little time, and I'm sure she'll be fine, just like you were." She wished she could be sure of it, though.

"What if she's not fine with it?" Jorie groaned. "I never thought about that. What if she can't accept this? Can't accept us?"

There was no easy answer. Helplessly, Griffin stared over Jorie's shoulder at her family.

They crowded around them in silent support.

Gus settled one hand on Jorie's shoulder while the other rested on Griffin's back.

"Come on," Nella said. "Let's clean the kitchen while we wait."

Griffin watched as the members of her family began to wash the dishes, stow away leftover food, and sweep the floor. She wrapped her arms more tightly around Jorie and looked around. "Where's Brian?"

"No idea," Jorie said. "Maybe he is getting some fresh air. I think he's still not over the shock of Mom thinking he is Gus's lover."

Come to think of it, Griffin hadn't seen him since they had left Helen in the living room. "Oh, no." She let go of Jorie and strode to the door.

Someone grabbed her arm.

Griffin whirled around.

"Leave them alone for a while longer," Gus said. "They're just talking."

Her sensitive hearing confirmed it. Brian's

calm voice rumbled through the living room, followed by Helen's higher-pitched tones. She didn't sound scared or threatened. In fact, Griffin heard her chuckle a time or two.

Used to respecting other people's privacy, Griffin turned her head away and returned to the kitchen.

"Everything okay?" Jorie asked. Concern reflected in her dark eyes. "Brian's not in there with Mom, is he?"

"Yes, he is." Griffin grabbed Jorie when she tried to hurry past her. "Don't worry. Gus is keeping an eye on them. And they're actually sounding pretty friendly. My father is using his feline charms on your mother."

"What?" Jorie still looked worried. "Since Gus is happily married to Martha, I assume you mean Brian?"

Griffin trailed her hands over Jorie's back in soothing circles. "I think your mother impressed him. Not that he would ever admit that a human—" She stopped midsentence and mentally repeated what Jorie had just said. Her throat constricted, and she gulped. "You know that moving in together makes the Kasari consider a couple married?"

Jorie nodded. "Ronnie told me when Leigh moved in with her."

"But...but..." Shock made Griffin's skin itch, but she quickly shook it off. "But that was before you asked me to move in with you."

Fine lines formed at the edges of Jorie's eyes when she smiled. "Somehow, asking you to move in seemed less scary then asking you to marry me." The smile vanished. "You're not angry with me for not telling you I knew what it meant?"

"Angry?" Griffin laughed and bent to kiss Jorie. "I was trying to figure out how to tell you that U-Haul jokes have a very different meaning for Wrasa."

Jorie laughed. "The bigger problem is how to tell my mom that I got married without her."

"Oh, Great Hunter." Griffin scratched her head.

"One family crisis at a time, sis," Kylin said as she and Rufus walked over. "While we're all here together, there's something we want to tell you." She hesitated and looked over at Rufus, who just grinned. "Remember how Helen thought Jorie was expecting the latest litter of Westmore cubs?"

Griffin rolled her eyes. "She's not pregnant."

"No." A grin lit up Kylin's face. "But I am."

"What?"

Still grinning madly, Kylin nodded.

"Oh. Oh, wow." Griffin wrapped her arms around her sister and whirled her around. Wild waves of happiness wafted up from Ky and mixed with the aroma of Griffin's own joy.

"Put my mate down!" A low growl rumbled through Rufus.

Griffin had never heard a sound like that from the usually quiet hybrid. Suddenly, she understood why he had refused to be the one to demonstrate shifting for Helen. As an expecting father, he was in a state of constant overprotective vigilance. She set Kylin back down but kept grinning at her. "This is so great. Congratulations. I always thought having children together wouldn't be possible for two hybrids."

"That's what we thought too," Kylin said quietly. Her amber eyes glowed like golden treasures.

"Yeah, well, apparently, this is one area where I'm more 'talented' than you, cat," Rufus said, using Gus's words. He regarded Griffin with a smug smile.

Wolf humor. Griffin's eyes narrowed. She shot him a fake threatening gaze. "Just be glad that you are the father of my future niece or nephew."

"Niece or nephew?" Gus rushed over to them.

Nella was hot on his heels. She stared at Kylin. "Does that mean...?"

Kylin nodded.

Chaos broke out in the kitchen as the family crowded around Kylin and Rufus, shouting questions.

"What's going on in here?" Brian boomed from the doorway. "Do you want Helen to think we're nothing but an uncivilized bunch of howling animals?" He stood with one hand on Helen's back.

"Do you want Helen to think we're a horde of uncaring monsters who don't even celebrate when they learn that their daughter is pregnant?" Gus shouted back.

Brian's hand slid from Helen's back. "Daughter? Pregnant?"

"Don't look at me," Leigh said. "No sperm in this relationship either."

"Ky?" Brian's booming voice was now a whisper.

Kylin nodded, the liger-size grin still on her face.

Brian stormed across the kitchen and whirled

Kylin around until Rufus growled at him too.

A shell-shocked Helen still stood in the doorway. "I think I need a drink."

"Sorry," Griffin said. "Wrasa can't drink alcohol, so we don't keep any in the house."

Jorie walked over to them. "I'm sorry we sprang this on you today, Mom, but I don't think there's an easy way to tell you that I'm married to a shape-shifter."

Married. Griffin flinched. They hadn't wanted to tell Helen that just yet. "Um, sweetie…"

But Helen just chuckled. "Relax. Brian already told me that his…his pride considers you married." She stood watching Kylin and Rufus for long minutes. "They look as happy as your father and I when we brought you home."

"Ky and Rufus always thought they weren't able to have children together," Jorie said. "They tried for over a year, but the Wrasa doctors didn't give them much hope."

Understanding shone in Helen's eyes.

Jorie's parents had gone through the same before adopting Jorie.

"The Wrasa…they are good people," Helen finally said.

"Most of them," Jorie answered. "Just like us humans."

Helen turned to Griffin. "I don't think we should have pasties together tomorrow morning."

An iron fist squeezed Griffin's heart. "Oh?"

"Judging from the way your family ate at dinner, I think we should go for bacon and sausages."

Relief swept through Griffin. She regarded Helen with a grateful gaze.

Jorie rushed into her mother's arms.

"You know, this was the weirdest Christmas I ever had." Helen sighed.

"Mine too," Griffin said.

Smiling, Jorie reached out and touched her hand. "This is the first Christmas you ever celebrated."

Still wrapped in Jorie's embrace, Helen turned toward Griffin. "You won't try to top this next year, will you?"

Griffin chuckled. "No."

The old warmth filled Helen's eyes when she extended one arm to include Griffin in the embrace. "Then Merry Christmas."

###

Babysitter Material

KYLIN PUT DOWN THE PHONE.

"And?" Eagerness lit up Rufus's brown eyes. "Will they take them?"

Ky sighed. "They can't. Jorie needs to meet with Jeff Madsen in Boise tomorrow evening, and Griff is going with her."

"Oh." Rufe's face fell. He gnawed on his lip. "Hm. Leigh and Rhonda still aren't back from their negotiations with the Canadian prides?"

"No. I bet it'll take all week. Remember that they are negotiating with a bunch of stubborn cats, not canines who can be bribed with—"

"Hey!" Rufus protested.

"—food and sex," Ky finished.

Rufus barked out a laugh.

Ky's tight lips eased into a smile. *Mission accomplished.* She had made him laugh and chased away the disappointment from his face, at least for a moment.

"If we can't find a babysitter, there's not going to be any food and sex for us," Rufe said. A sigh tousled a lock of thick, brown hair that fell onto Rufus's forehead. "At least not as part of a nice evening with a romantic dinner for two and a long run through the forest."

He was right. It seemed they'd have to spend their two-year anniversary at home. Ky longed for some uninterrupted time alone with Rufe, but even after moving to Michigan, it wasn't always easy to find someone with enough time and energy to take the triplets off their hands for a few hours. It felt like months since they had last run through the forest together in their animal forms. Just the thought of it made her blood sing with the rush of the hunt.

A loud wail interrupted her daydream.

"That's Ry," Rufus said. "I'll go."

Seconds later, Kylin heard him talk to their six-month-old son. Contented babbling answered.

Ky grinned. He was such a good father. She wondered whether her own fathers had ever talked to her like that when she had been a cub. Had Brian and Gus even seen her every now and then when she had been that age?

A sudden thought shot through her. *It's crazy.* Then a broad grin darted across her face. *But why not?* "Rufe," she called over to the nursery. "We could call my fathers and ask them to babysit."

Silence answered her. Even Ry's babbling stopped for a moment. "Great Hunter, no. I just got used to being a father. I don't want to lose them this soon." She heard Rufus blow raspberries over the baby's skin. "We won't throw you to the big, mean lions, will we, Ry?"

Ky laughed. "It won't be so bad. My fathers are big softies at heart."

"I'm not worried about Gus, but Brian is not babysitter material." Rufe wandered into the living room, bouncing Ryan on his hip. "I bet he'll say no anyway."

"What if he says yes?"

"He won't."

"But if he does?" Ky asked.

In the nursery, Quinn began to cry. Mia immediately joined in.

Rufus grinned. "Then he's in for quite a surprise, and we get to celebrate our anniversary in style."

"You agreed to do what?" Slack-jawed, Gus stared at his brother.

"I hear humans call it babysitting," Brian said.

"Babysitting? You?" Gus drew out the pronoun as if it had at least twenty syllables.

His brother's wide-eyed amazement rankled Brian. "Why not? They're just little cubs, so they'll probably sleep the whole time anyway. How hard can it be?"

Gus just laughed.

Narrowing his eyes to his most intimidating glare, Brian glowered at him. "We're ruling a pride. We're descendants of a long line of proud Kasari alphas. Why shouldn't we be able to keep three little cubs in line for a few hours?"

"When was the last time you babysat, Brian?"

"We have three daughters, and they all turned out pretty well." Brian's chest swelled with pride.

Gus snorted. "You weren't around when Ky and Griff were babies, and Leigh...she spent more time at Martha's house than over here when she was growing up."

The truth of his words pierced Brian with

merciless claws. He ducked his head but then straightened. "I probably wasn't the best father," he said, his voice low. "But now is our chance to do better with our grandchildren. So are you in or not?"

"Of course I'm in." Gus grinned from ear to ear. "The great Brian Eldridge changing diapers and burping his grandkids. Wouldn't want to miss that."

Brian blanched.

∝◡

They look so small. So helpless. Brian's protective instincts flared as he stared down into the collapsible baby bed that Kylin and Rufus had carried into the house twenty minutes ago. The three babies were sleeping, snuggled up to each other like lion cubs. *And they're handsome.* That was a given, of course. They were his grandchildren after all.

Gus leaned over Brian's shoulder to watch the babies too.

"See?" With a satisfied grin, Brian pointed at the sleeping children. "Nothing to this babysitting stuff."

One of the babies opened its amber eyes. It glanced around until its gaze landed on Brian.

Brian grinned down at the baby. "Hey there, cub."

The baby scrunched up its face and started to cry. The shrill noise woke up baby number two, who promptly started to wail too. Seconds later, all three of them were crying at a volume that made Brian's eardrums vibrate.

"Yup," Gus said. "Nothing to it at all. Want me to call Martha and ask her to come over?"

"No!" No one would ever be able to say that Brian Eldridge, ruling alpha of the Ottawa National Forest pride, wasn't able to keep his grandchildren in line and had to call for help. *But, Great Hunter, they're loud! How can someone with such tiny lungs cry so loudly?* Brian covered his sensitive ears. *What now?* He tried to remember what he had done when Leigh had cried. *I woke up Leigh's mother. All right, I wasn't exactly father of the year, but that was then and this is now.* A brilliant idea popped into his mind. "Time for a bedtime story." He rubbed his hands and bent over the bed so that they would be able to hear him over their incessant crying. "Once upon a time, there were three little Kasari cubs. They lived deep in the woods. One day, they decided—"

"Brian." Gus cleared his voice. "This is not a children's story. Don't you remember what happens when the humans find the three little cubs?"

"They don't understand what I'm saying anyway," Brian answered. He turned back toward the babies. "So, the little cubs decided to visit—"

"No." Gus pulled on Brian's arm until Brian looked up and glared at him. "These three are not going to grow up seeing humans as enemies. This is a new era, and they are part of a new generation. Get used to it."

Annoyance prickled along Brian's skin. *Okay, so no bedtime story. What then? Ah!* He opened his mouth and started to sing. He didn't remember the complete lyrics of the annoying human cartoon movie, but the line about "the lion sleeps tonight" sounded good to him.

Not to the cubs, apparently. They started to wail even louder.

Frustrated, Brian stopped his singing and let out a growl.

The crying stopped. Wide-eyed, the babies stared up at Brian.

"Uh-oh! Now you've done it," Gus said. "You scared them."

One of the babies let out a delighted laugh.

Brian blinked. Just to test it out, he growled again.

Baby number two and three giggled.

"Ha!" Brian grinned proudly. "They like that. They are Kasari, so they're not afraid of a little growling."

Baby number one pulled itself up into a sitting position and reached its little arms out.

Not sure what the kid wanted, Brian bent down.

Small hands grabbed his beard and pulled.

"Ouch." Brian flinched back and growled.

The beard-pulling baby clapped its hands and laughed.

"Oh, yeah." Gus chuckled. "Nothing to this babysitting stuff at all."

The spoon landed in the baby food with a splash. The gooey stuff splattered all over Brian's shirt. He grimaced.

Across the table, sitting on Gus's lap, baby number two was busy dripping juice all over its chin and down on the table.

Ugh. Brian's neat cat side shivered inwardly. "Are we sure they are Kylin's?"

"Maybe they take after their father," Gus

said while he tried to convince the child on his lap to hold the cup with both hands. "It'll be interesting to see what they'll be able to turn into once they grow up."

"This one's going to be a coyote," Brian said, nodding down at the kid who was scratching at his pant leg like a coyote digging for leftover food.

"She just wants you to lift her up on your lap."

Brian looked at the kid already sitting on his lap. *Ah, well. The shirt's already ruined.* He bent down and settled baby number three on his free thigh. A horrible stench drifted up to Brian's nose. He sniffed carefully, first one baby, then the other. *Ugh. They both stink.* "Uh, Gus..."

Gus barely looked up. He was busy bouncing the baby on his lap. "What?"

"I think these two need their diapers changed." Brian wrinkled his sensitive nose.

"Yeah, little Mia too. You do remember how, don't you?"

"Of course I do." Wrapping a diaper around a baby's behind couldn't be so hard, could it? Two brilliant doctors who performed complicated, life-saving surgeries for a living should be able to figure it out. "All right. Let's do this." Brian stood and plopped one of the kids down on Gus's lap. "You take baby number one and number two. I'll take baby number three."

"Why do I have to change two?" Gus asked.

"Because I'm the dominant alpha."

"Ha! Coward." Grumbling, Gus followed him into the living room. "And besides, they have names, you know? They're not just baby number one, two, and three."

Brian peeked at his brother and imitated his moves when Gus pulled off the babies' little pants. "They all look alike. How do you tell them apart?"

"They don't look alike at all." Gus took off his babies' soiled diapers.

Brian followed suit and pinched his nose at the stench.

"Quinn is the one with the reddish hair," Gus said. "Mia's eyes are green. And Ryan, the one you have, is the only boy—which is why you should cover him up after you take off his diaper, or he'll..."

A stream of warm liquid trickled over Brian's shirt.

"Ooops." Gus laughed. "Too late. Sorry, brother."

Half an hour later, babies and Brian freshly changed, they settled down on one of the rugs in the living room for some playtime. Brian handed them the rattles and toys that Kylin and Rufus had left, but the babies weren't interested in them. They kept escaping from the rug to explore the living room. Even crawling on hands and knees, the babies were amazingly fast.

"Oh, no." Brian caught one of the kids as it made a beeline to his desk. "This is my territory, and that is yours. Back on the rug you go." He settled down on the rug and stretched out his long legs to both sides, forming a fence to keep the children away from his desk. Pain flared up his foot. "Ouch!"

The kid with the green eyes looked up at

him, still gnawing on his socked foot.

"Gus!" Brian gestured. "Make it stop!"

Laughing, Gus lifted the baby away. He rolled onto his back and settled the kid on his chest. He put a finger in her mouth. "She's just teething. Chewing seems to soothe the pain."

"Not mine." Brian rubbed his toe.

"Brian," Gus shouted and pointed wildly.

A smug grin spread over Brian's face. "What? Is the kid biting you too?"

"No! Stop her!"

Brian whirled around.

The redheaded kid had crawled into the forbidden territory and reached for the cord of Brian's printer.

Brian lunged across the room and snatched up the baby just before the printer could topple from its shelf—and on top of the baby.

Clutched in Brian's arms, the baby stared for a moment and then started to wail.

The noise vibrated through Brian's bones. "Forget about wondering what kind of shifter they'll be as adults. If they continue to be that annoying, they won't make it to puberty." Brian's heart pounded in his ears. He let out a deep, rumbling growl.

The red-haired baby stopped crying and laughed in delight. It threw its small arms around Brian's neck and said, "Baba!"

The growl died in Brian's throat. His heart melted. "Did you hear that?"

"What?"

"The baby...it...she said 'baba'—that clearly means Grandpa."

Gus smirked. "Clearly."

The baby patted Brian's cheeks. "Baba," it

repeated.

"See?" Brian's chest swelled. "She means me. She knows I'm her grandfather." Babysitting his grandchildren wasn't so bad after all. There clearly was a bond between him and the kids. He purred in contentment.

"Yes, dear, whatever you say."

"Will wonders never cease?" Rufus looked into the rearview mirror. Ry and Mia slept peacefully while Quinn studied her fingers. They were diapered, fed, and happy. "I thought Brian would greet us at the door, ready to hand over the children as quickly as possible." He'd clearly underestimated his father-in-law. The old lion seemed to have fallen in love with his grandchildren.

"I'll call Gus later," Kylin said. "I'm sure he'll tell us how the triplets managed to wrap Dad around their little fingers."

Rufus halted the car at a red light. A family walking a dog crossed the street in front of them.

In the backseat, Quinn pointed excitedly at the large, black dog. "Baba!"

"Dog," Kylin said.

Quinn pointed again. "Baba."

Rufus shrugged and leaned over to kiss Kylin. "Happy anniversary."

###

When the Cat's Away

AJARRING SCREAM WOKE GRIFFIN from her catnap.

Jorie! Griffin leaped from the bed and bounded to the living room, where the scream had come from. A fierce hiss rose from her chest, and a burning sensation flared along her skin as her need to shift increased. Ready to protect her mate against any danger, she burst through the door.

The sight before her made her slide to a stop. Squinting, she took in the scene in the living room.

There was no attacker and no visible danger. Jorie's coconut-and-forest scent was the only human smell in the room. Griffin's gaze slid over Jorie, taking in every inch of her.

Jorie sat in front of her laptop, her bare feet tucked beneath her and the sleeves of Griffin's favorite shirt rolled up a few times to keep them from hanging over her fingers. Her gleaming black hair, disheveled as if she had run her hands through it, fell into a paler than usual face.

"Hey," Griffin said. "Everything okay?"

Jorie's scent said something had startled

her, but the odor of fear was missing. Her eyes wide and darkened to black, Jorie stared at her and pointed to something on the floor.

Griffin looked down.

A handful of blue, green, red, and yellow M&M's dotted the floor. A brown one peeked out from beneath the coffee table, and another one rested against Griffin's foot. She bent and picked up Jorie's favorite candy. Grinning, she leaned against the doorway. "Lost your marbles, darling?"

Jorie scowled and pointed in the general direction of her desk. "It was the mouse."

Ah, so that was the problem. Jorie had fiddled with the piece of technology and knocked over the candy jar she kept on her desk. Always willing to help her mate with her writing in whatever way she could, Griffin strode over and picked up the mouse. She gave it an experimental shake and clicked the two buttons. "Maybe it's the batteries."

"No." Jorie took the mouse away from Griffin and set it back on her desk.

"No? You already put in new batteries?"

"There is a mouse behind my desk," Jorie said, speaking slowly and pronouncing every syllable as if Griffin wouldn't understand otherwise. She pointed again.

This time, Griffin realized she was pointing to something beneath the desk. "A mouse? In my territory? I mean...in our house? Are you sure?" Surely none of the tiny beasts would dare enter the den of a liger-shifter.

"Oh, yeah. It tried to stick its wriggling nose into my candy jar, and when I screamed, it disappeared behind the desk. Now it's hiding somewhere." Black hair flew as Jorie shook her head. "I live with four cats. Four! And one of them is a 400-pound liger. Yet not one of you is able to catch one lousy mouse?"

When she put it like that, it sounded pretty pathetic.

Will, the red tomcat, lolloped into the room and sniffed the M&Ms. One of the other cats, Emmy, wandered in too. She circled Griffin once, leaving behind a trail of tri-colored hair on Griffin's sweatpants, before she strode toward the kitchen.

"Don't look at us like that," Griffin said. She bent and picked up Will, who pushed his head beneath her chin and purred. His whiskers tickled and made Griffin smile. "Will here only's got three paws, so that disqualifies him from mouse-hunting."

"Oh, is that so?" Jorie got up and sashayed over. Her enchanting scent made Griffin's heartbeat speed up as Jorie reached over to scratch Will behind one ear. "What's your excuse, then? Last night, all your paws were in full working order."

A purr rumbled up Griffin's chest as she remembered. She grinned and playfully covered Will's ears with her hand. "Not in front of the cats, darling."

Jorie laughed and leaned forward to kiss Griffin.

With the cat purring between them, Griffin finally broke the kiss. "If you didn't have an open jar of candy by your desk, maybe the mouse would have stayed outside, where it belongs."

"But my brain needs the sugar while I'm writing," Jorie said, arms folded.

Two years of living with a writer had taught Griffin not to argue against it. "Then maybe you should at least allow cats in the room while you write. That would prevent cheeky rodents from taking up residence in the living room."

"Oh, no, that's not negotiable. If I didn't declare the living room a cat-free zone every now and then, I'd never get any writing done. You are much too distracting."

Griffin proved her right by putting Will down, pulling Jorie into her arms, and stealing another kiss.

"So, what are you gonna do?" Jorie asked when they came up for air.

"Do?" Purring, Griffin nibbled on Jorie's bottom lip. "I thought I could do more of this..." She gave the corner of Jorie's mouth a teasing lick. "And this..." Another kiss nearly made her lose her train of thought.

After long seconds, Jorie, now clinging to Griffin, wrenched her lips away. "No, I mean... what are you gonna do about the mouse?"

Griffin thought about it, sorting through different hunting strategies in her mind. If the coward of a mouse was hiding behind the desk, a frontal attack wouldn't work, and an all-out hunt would be too hard on Jorie's furniture. Clearly, the situation demanded a more subtle tactic. "I'll call my fathers and have them come over to help."

Jorie slid her gaze up Griffin's solid six-foot-two frame. "You need help to catch one tiny mouse?"

"Hey, you are the one who constantly encourages me to explore my Kasari side. I'm half lion. We hunt in prides. And my fathers have lived in Michigan much longer than me. They know the local prey." Griffin gave her partner a confident grin. "One mouse. Three cat-shifters. Do the math. The house will be a rodent-free zone in no time."

Brian was silent for several seconds. "Say that again."

Griffin's lips tightened. She pressed the phone closer to her ear and peeked left and right, making sure that no one, not even the cats, could witness her embarrassing admission. Thankfully, Jorie had left for her monthly reading at the local library. "I'm in the doghouse with Jorie because there's a mouse in the living room."

Her father roared with laughter.

"Thank you very much for your overwhelming show of compassion," Griffin said. "And here I thought you'd want to help me."

Brian's laughter died down. "I do, Griffin. Really. Gus and I will be over in a minute. After all, we can't have Jorie thinking our daughter isn't a good mouser. Want us to bring the pride?"

"Um. No. That would be overkill."

"All right. Gus, get over here. We need to go over to Jorie and Griffin's. Their house is overrun with mice." Brian's voice boomed, loud enough for half the pride to hear him.

Groaning, Griffin pressed the end button and covered her eyes with her hand. "The house isn't overrun. It's just one tiny little mouse." At least, that's what she hoped. If the mouse had family, her reputation was toast. She glared at the desk, where Jorie had last seen the mouse.

"Prepare to be annihilated. Resistance is futile."

Stealthily, the three cat-shifters prowled into the living room. In the middle of the room, they fanned out. Griffin patrolled the area in front of the tall bookshelf. Gus took up position next to the easy chair, while Brian advanced into enemy territory toward the desk.

Not moving a claw, they waited.

And waited.

Griffin shifted her weight from one foot to the other, but she bravely stood by her post.

"I know cats are supposed to be patient," Gus said beneath his breath, "but that's because humans think we have nine lives, so we have time to spare. Even if we had, I wouldn't want to waste one of them sitting around, waiting for a mouse to make an appearance."

At the sound of Gus's deep voice, something moved beneath the desk, half hidden in the jungle of power cords.

Brian lunged forward.

The mouse squeaked and scampered out from beneath the desk. A shadow darted past Griffin.

She pounced.

But a cramped living room was not the place for three cat-shifters to go on a big-game hunt. Gus, his feet tangled in Jorie's comforter, crashed into her as he, too, tried to catch the mouse.

Griffin fell. The corner of the coffee table scraped along her forehead. Pain shot through her, and she snarled as the tiny hairs on her arms lengthened. *No!* Jorie's rules were as strict as her fathers' had been when she was a teenager—no shifting indoors. By the time Griffin had fought down the urge to shift, a tiny tail disappeared behind the bookcase. She sank against the coffee table and rubbed her forehead. "Oh, yeah. The house will be a rodent-free zone in no time."

"It has to come out of there sometime, right?" Brian said as they took up position in front of the bookcase.

Griffin lifted a brow at him. "Yeah, but not before Jorie comes back from her author's reading. Do you want to be the one to explain to Jorie why three cat-shifters failed to catch the mouse?"

Crawling closer on hands and knees, Gus peered behind the bookcase. "What if one of us reaches behind the bookcase? Even if we can't get a hold of the mouse, it might chase the damn thing out from behind the bookcase."

Griffin nodded. It sounded like a reasonable hunting strategy. But the thought of sliding her hand through all the dust and spiderwebs behind the bookcase made her wrinkle her nose. She looked at Gus, who looked at Brian.

"Fine." Brian growled. "I'll do it. Get out of the way, you scaredy-cats." He squeezed between the desk and the bookcase and, looking as if he were smelling five-day-old fish, slid his hand along the wall.

Gus and Griffin took up position on the other end of the bookcase, ready to pounce should the mouse show its muzzle.

Something rustled.

Griffin shifted her weight. The suspense made the skin of her arms tingle. "Do you have it?"

"Hold on," Brian said, up to his shoulder behind the bookcase now. "I've got it! I've got it! I've got...something." He pulled his prey out from behind the bookcase.

Griffin dashed over.

But the thing in Brian's hand wasn't a mouse. There, on Brian's dust-covered palm, lay a blue M&M. With a snort, Brian threw the candy over his shoulder.

Emmy wandered in and pounced on the rolling candy, hunting it as it ricocheted all over the living room.

"If you want to hunt something, hunt that damn mouse," Brian told the cat.

Naturally, Emmy didn't listen. On her hunt for the M&M, she toppled over the research books Jorie had stacked next to the couch.

"I think it's time for a new strategy," Gus said. He plucked spiderwebs from his brother's sleeve and handed Griffin a tissue for the bleeding scratch on her forehead. "Have you tried a mousetrap?"

"Mousetrap?" Brian looked at him as if Gus had suggested using a flame-thrower in Jorie's living room.

Gus shrugged. "Why not? There's more than one way to skin a...uh...mouse."

Brian put his hands on his hips. "We come from a long line of successful hunters. We don't need those human contraptions. We can catch the damn mouse without a trap."

A tiny nose with quivering whiskers stuck

out from behind the bookcase, then quickly disappeared again as the mouse realized the siege was still ongoing.

"If my reputation as a hunter wasn't at risk, I'd almost find it...cute," Griffin said.

"Cute?" Brian roared.

"In a totally preylike way, of course," Griffin said. "So, what do we do now?"

When Griffin heard Jorie's car rumble down the street, she stood holding Jorie's prized lesbian fiction award, protecting the fragile teardrop-shaped glass while Gus stacked one pile of books after the other on the coffee table and Brian tried to move the bookcase.

Griffin's gaze darted around the living room. She took in the toppled-over stack of research books, the blood-dotted tissue on the coffee table, and the trampled remains of an M&M on the floor. The living room looked as if a war had been waged there.

A war that the mouse was still winning.

Just as Jorie's key jangled at the front door, Brian finally managed to move the bookcase.

"Quick," Gus called, his eyes glowing with hunting fever.

Griffin put the award down on the couch and tensed her muscles, ready to pounce.

The door to the living room opened.

Griffin looked up and met Jorie's wide-eyed gaze. Out of the corner of her eye, she saw the mouse dash behind the desk.

With a careful zigzag course, Jorie climbed over the various obstacles. "What's going on here?"

"Um, nothing much. How was the reading?" Griffin lifted her upper lip to let Jorie's scent brush over the roof of her mouth. Her knotted muscles relaxed as the scent didn't bring the image of storm-whipped trees. *She's not angry.*

"It went fine, but I think that's more than can be said about this." Jorie pointed at her rearranged living room. She brushed her lips over Griffin's, then pulled back to take in the scratch on her forehead. "What happened to you?"

"Oh, it's nothing."

Brian rubbed at a speck of dust on his sleeve. "Hey, kitten. Did you know that it's really dusty behind your bookcase?"

"I can see that." Jorie walked over and plucked a bit of spiderweb from Brian's beard, then leaned over to kiss his cheek.

"Yes, but we took care of it for you." Gus stretched his neck to receive his own kiss.

"Thank you so much, kind sir." The corner of Jorie's mouth twitched. "But what about the mouse? Did you catch it?"

Gus held up his hands. "One project after the other." He sauntered to the door. "Do you, by any chance, have cheese in the fridge?"

Griffin got into the car. Fiddling with her seat belt, she glanced into the rearview mirror. "You can say it. Don't hold back on my part. I know you think I'm a lousy mouser."

The silence from the backseat sounded like a confirmation.

"I know what you're thinking. A 400-pound

liger should be able to hunt down a little mouse, right?"

No objection came from the backseat.

"But you should keep in mind that my weight and height actually has me at a disadvantage. I can't just squeeze behind the bookcase, and—"

The door on the passenger side opened, and Jorie climbed in. "Who are you talking to?"

"Um. No one."

Jorie grinned and gently poked her. "You were talking to the mouse."

"Please." Griffin threw a glance over her shoulder to the backseat, where the mouse scurried around in the cage of the live catch trap. "That's ridiculous."

"Don't worry. I won't tell anyone that big, bad Griffin Westmore has a heart as soft as a marshmallow."

Griffin grumbled.

After turning in her seat, Jorie caressed Griffin's cheek and guided her head around until Griffin met her gaze. "Stop pouting already. I don't care that you're not the fiercest mouser in Michigan. I didn't marry you for your hunting skills."

"No?" Under the heat of Jorie's gaze, Griffin began to purr. "Then why did you marry me?"

A grin spread over Jorie's face. "Because I can't cook to save my life, and you saved me from starvation or food poisoning, whatever would have come first."

"You!" With a playful snarl, Griffin whirled around and dug her fingers into Jorie's vulnerable sides, making her squeak along with the mouse in the backseat. When Jorie's bursts of laughter finally died down, Griffin gentled her touch and kissed her. If she couldn't be Michigan's best mouser, she'd at least be the best kisser.

Finally, Jorie moved back an inch and whispered against Griffin's lips, "I married you because you have a heart as soft as a marshmallow."

Purring, Griffin started the car to drive the mouse to its new home, far away from their house.

"But as much as I love you," Jorie said as they left Osgrove behind, "if we ever have another mouse, I'll call an exterminator."

###

Plus One

TAKING A BIG BITE OF her sandwich, Griffin stepped out of the kitchen.

A white object bounced against her shoes and ricocheted across the living room. Two cats skidded over the wood floor, nearly crashing into Griffin in their haste to be the one to catch their prey.

"Slow down, girls." Griffin wagged her finger at them. "You know the rules. No hunting indoors."

As usual, Agatha and Emmy ignored her orders and continued their hunt.

Will jumped down from the couch on his three paws to see what had captured the attention of the other cats.

"Not you too, Will." But finally, her curiosity got the better of Griffin, and she circled the coffee table.

Agatha was lying on her side, all claws digging into a crumpled sheet of paper. Emmy pounced to steal the paper ball from her, and the wild chase all over the living room resumed.

Griffin would have left the cats to their game, but she had learned that when you lived with a writer, a crumpled sheet of paper was never just a crumpled sheet of paper. It might be part of a scene that Jorie had thought wasn't working but would later decide to use anyway.

Always willing to be Jorie's champion, Griffin dove into the battle.

Before Griffin could reach the desired object, Emmy batted at it with one paw. The paper ball rolled beneath the couch. Emmy dashed after it, closely followed by Agatha.

Great. If Griffin reached beneath the couch, chances were that the cats, caught in their hunting fever, would forget who the top cat in the house was and scratch or bite her. *Time for a smarter hunting strategy.* Griffin knelt next to the couch, pinched off a bit of the turkey from her sandwich, and threw it under the couch. A few seconds later, she held out a second piece.

Emmy's tri-colored muzzle stuck out from beneath the couch, quivering as she inhaled the scent of the turkey.

Griffin dropped the piece of turkey two feet in front of the couch.

Emmy scrambled out from under the couch and gulped down the turkey.

Grinning, Griffin threw another bit of turkey across the room, luring Emmy farther away from the sheet of paper. She tried to repeat her trick with Agatha, but the red Somali cat didn't fall for it. She stayed beneath the couch, ignoring the turkey. Rustling sounds indicated that she was manhandling Jorie's paper.

Griffin suppressed a growl. She ripped the front page off the TV listing, crumpled it up, and tossed it toward the easy chair.

Agatha dashed out of her hiding place, this time hunting after the colorful paper ball.

Ha! The prey is mine! Griffin reached beneath the couch and extracted the sheet of paper. She sat on the couch, took another bite of her sandwich, and unfolded the crumpled page.

"Meow!" Emmy sat in front of her, her gaze directed at the sandwich in Griffin's hand. "Mrrraow!"

"Okay, okay. Tone it down, all right? I heard you the first time." Griffin handed over another hunk of turkey and gulped down the rest of her now nearly turkey-free sandwich. Good thing her fathers couldn't see her. Losing most of her lunch to a miniature tiger was embarrassing. But at least she had proven to be the superior hunter when it came to the paper ball. Carefully, she smoothed the creases from the paper and put on her reading glasses to decipher the typed words.

It wasn't one of Jorie's scenes. *Wonderful. I sacrificed half of my turkey for a piece of garbage.* Then she took a second glance. The wrinkled paper was a letter. Jorie's name caught her attention, and she continued to read.

Dear Marjorie,
The faculty and alumni of New Milford High School cordially invite you and a guest to join the rest of your classmates for your fifteen-year reunion. When: Saturday, August 17, 2013, 7 p.m. Where: Meridian Hotel. Cost: $40.00 per person. Please RSVP by Friday, August 2. We sincerely hope you will be able to make it!
Heather and Thomas Welkins

Griffin glanced at the big cat calendar on the wall. *August 17? That's in two weeks.* Why hadn't Jorie mentioned her high school reunion?

With Emmy trailing after her, Griffin stood and walked over to the bedroom. "Jorie?" She slowly opened the door.

Jorie was sitting on the bed, leaning against the headboard, her laptop balanced on her knees.

"Are you writing?" Griffin asked. While what Jorie was doing might seem like sitting around, staring at the laptop screen to others, Griffin knew writing was Jorie's job, and she always tried to be respectful of that.

Jorie looked up. "No, just surfing the web."

Griffin slipped into the room and stretched out on the bed next to Jorie.

Immediately, Jorie put the laptop on the floor and cuddled close with her head on Griffin's shoulder.

Jorie's scent normally made Griffin feel as if she were lying in a sun-dappled clearing, but today, Jorie's scent evoked mental images of clouds blocking out the sun. Griffin lifted her hand and combed her fingers through Jorie's hair. "Are you okay?"

Jorie buried her face more fully against Griffin's shoulder and nodded.

Griffin knew better than to believe it. "Bad dream?"

Her face still pressed against Griffin's shoulder, Jorie shook her head. "No," she said, her voice muffled. "The nightmares finally stopped."

"Thank the Great Hunter." Griffin stroked Jorie's head. "What is it, then? Is this about the high school reunion?"

Jorie stiffened in her arms. Slowly, she

looked up. "How do you know about that?"

"The cats couldn't keep their muzzles shut." At Jorie's puzzled expression, Griffin added, "They were chasing the invitation all over the living room. Why did you throw it away?"

"You know me." Jorie sat up, instantly making Griffin miss the body contact. "Parties are not my thing."

Griffin studied her. "This isn't just any party, though. Aren't you curious to find out what became of your classmates?"

Jorie tapped Griffin's nose. "Hasn't anyone ever told you that curiosity killed the cat?"

"You know what they say. We have nine lives," Griffin said. "And besides, you're human, not a cat. Aren't humans supposed to be eager to find out whether Mr. Most Likely to Serve Time in Prison really went down that career path? Or whether Ms. Most Likely to Get Pregnant during Spring Break has a gaggle of kids?"

"Not me. I was glad to leave high school behind, and I have no desire to relive those days." Jorie picked up her laptop and set her fingers on the keyboard as if getting ready to write.

Griffin could tell that her mind wasn't on writing, though. The stale scent of old pain clung to Jorie. "What did they do to you? They weren't the kids who put you in the goose enclosure, were they?"

"No, that was in middle school. High school kids have more subtle ways to make you suffer."

A protective snarl vibrated through Griffin's body. "What did they do?"

"Not much. Most of the time, they completely ignored my existence. I was never invited to any of the cool parties or just to hang out at the mall."

Griffin raised her brows. "Did you want to do that?"

"No, but it still would have been nice to be asked, you know? All I wanted back then was to fit in—to be normal. But then I made the mistake of letting one of the popular girls read a short story I had written about the creatures from my dreams." Jorie drew in a shaky breath. "She ridiculed me, calling the story childish. The next day, someone had spray-painted 'weirdo' on my locker."

Holding back a growl, Griffin engulfed her in an embrace and pushed the laptop off Jorie's lap to be closer. "Clueless kids. They had no idea how special you are." She peppered kisses along Jorie's neck and collarbone, putting every bit of love and admiration in each kiss.

Finally, Jorie relaxed in her arms.

"No wonder you never want to see any of your classmates again," Griffin said. "Assholes."

"Actually..." Jorie stared off into space, and then a small smile darted across her face. The scent of her pain faded away. "There's one or two I'd like to see. One of them even repainted my locker for me."

"Then maybe you should go and find out how he's doing," Griffin said.

"She," Jorie said. "But I don't know. Going all the way to Connecticut on the off chance that the few people I'd like to see will be there..." She narrowed her eyes. "You're not exactly a party animal either. Why the sudden interest in my high school reunion?"

"I'm not interested in your reunion—I'm

interested in you," Griffin said. "I have a feeling you have some unfinished business, and the reunion might be a chance to let go of it."

Jorie pulled the notebook back on her lap and rubbed her fingers over the touchpad. "Maybe you're right. It's just..."

Griffin slid off the bed, placed the laptop back on Jorie's lap, and bent to press a kiss to Jorie's lowered head. "Give it some thought, okay? I'll support you in whatever you decide." She left the bedroom, closed the door behind her, and stood listening for a moment.

No sounds of typing came from the other side of the door. "Griffin?" Jorie called after a moment, knowing Griffin with her Wrasa hearing could hear her even from the living room.

Griffin opened the door. "Yes?"

"All right. I'll go," Jorie said from her place on the bed. "On one condition."

"Okay. I'll make lasagna tonight and then let you have your way with the cook."

A pillow sailed through the air and hit the half-open door. "That's not what I meant. I want you to be my plus one and attend the reunion with me."

Griffin gulped. An evening in a banquet room full of humans showing off photos of their cubs was not her idea of fun. "Are you sure you wouldn't rather have the lasagna and a night of hot, wild—"

A second pillow hit her in the face. "Who says I can't have both?"

Griffin marched back into the bedroom and closed the door behind her. On her way over to the bed, she stripped off her shirt. "Certainly not me."

~~~

"Three?" The flight attendant's eyes bulged. "Did you just say you wanted three snack boxes and three sandwiches?"

"Something wrong with that?" Griffin asked. *Don't complain, or I might order three flight attendants to go along with that, sweetheart.* Part of her wanted to unfold her six-foot-two frame and stare down at the woman until she ran to get her lunch. Normally, she had better control over such impulses, but flying always put her in a bad mood. Being forced to wedge her tall body into a seat designed for midgets didn't help either.

Next to her, Jorie looked up from her laptop and patted Griffin's leg. "She's a big girl."

"Of course," the flight attendant said. "I just wanted to make sure." She fled down the aisle.

Griffin's gaze followed her the way she would track a fleeing deer.

Jorie reached over and slapped her thigh. "Behave. What is it with you and service personnel? Roberta, the waitress in the diner, still seems a bit scared of you too. I hope you'll hide your predatory side better at the reunion."

"I'll be a real pussy cat," Griffin said, grinning. She leaned back and tried to get comfortable in the airplane seat.

In record time, the flight attendant returned with their food.

Jorie rifled through Griffin's snack boxes and helped herself to the chocolate chip cookies.

Griffin didn't mind. Chocolate had a poisonous effect on Wrasa anyway. While a few cookies wouldn't kill her, they would make her queasy. She unwrapped the first sandwich, lifted one side of the bread, and flicked a piece of lettuce aside. Her mouth watered as the smell of juicy ham drifted up. It wasn't exactly gourmet food, but still good enough. She took the first bite and chewed slowly. "So," she said after swallowing, "want to give me a list of the asses you need me to kick tonight?"

Jorie licked a bit of chocolate off her fingers, a sight that momentarily made Griffin forget her sandwich. "You're going to the reunion as my girlfriend, not my bodyguard, remember?"

"I know." Jorie was fiercely independent, and Griffin didn't want her any other way, but she couldn't change her protectiveness any more than she could change the stripes of her liger form. Still, the thought of teaching Jorie's tormentors a lesson was tempting. "Any asses I need to kick as your girlfriend? An old date who might still have a crush on you? Or someone who broke your heart when you were a teenager?"

Jorie unwrapped her next cookie and shook her head. "I didn't date in high school."

Griffin paused with the second sandwich halfway to her mouth. "Not even once?"

"No. I just wasn't interested, and no one was interested in me."

"Wonderful." Griffin rolled her eyes. "We'll spend the evening with a bunch of stupid people."

A smile spread over Jorie's face, and she leaned over to kiss Griffin's cheek. "Charmer."

Twenty minutes later, the "fasten seat belt" sign came on. Griffin swallowed the last crumb of her third sandwich and stuffed the rest of the snack boxes into Jorie's laptop case. "For later."

Jorie sent her an amused glance. "I'm sure there'll be food at the reunion."

Griffin shrugged. "You never know. I have a feeling I'm gonna need the energy."

When they pulled into the hotel's parking lot, Jorie looked out the passenger side window of their rental car and groaned. "Christ, there are mini vans everywhere. I hope you're prepared to look at a lot of children's photos." She fidgeted with the seatbelt before finally managing to strip it off.

Griffin stopped her from opening the door with a touch to Jorie's leg. "Are you nervous?" she asked, even though her nose already told her the answer.

Jorie started to shake her head but then paused. "Maybe a little."

"We can leave at any time," Griffin said.

"Not exactly. We booked a room at the hotel, remember?"

Griffin gave a sheepish grin. "Then we'll just sneak upstairs and have our own private prom night."

"Don't tempt me," Jorie said.

"Maybe I shouldn't have talked you into coming here." Griffin searched Jorie's face. Had she made a mistake that would end up hurting Jorie even more?

"I admit that I'd rather be home with you," Jorie said. "But you were right. This is a chance to prove to myself that the stupid high school kids can't hurt me anymore. I've outgrown them."

Griffin leaned across the middle console and kissed her. "You did. Let's go in."

Half an hour later, after they had checked in, taken a shower, and changed, a hotel employee directed them toward the banquet room. A banner reading "Welcome New Milford High grads" greeted them. In front of the door to the banquet room, a table with nametags had been set up.

The brunette woman behind the table was wearing a ball gown and pearls that looked as if they cost more than Griffin made in a year.

Griffin glanced down at her black slacks and emerald shirt that Jorie loved because, as she said, it contrasted so nicely with her hair color. *Wow, she takes overdressed to a whole new level.*

"Wait, don't tell me." Beaming, the woman tilted her head and studied Jorie. "I know you, right? You were the girl who had the lead in the play we did our junior year. What was your name again? Melissa?"

Jorie somehow managed not to flinch. "Jorie...Marjorie Price. And no, I wasn't one of the actors. I wrote the script of the play."

"Oh, right," the brunette said, but the furrows on her forehead revealed that she still had no clue who Jorie was. She handed Jorie her nametag and directed her gaze at Griffin. "And you? I don't think you were in our class, were you? Are you someone's wife?"

Jorie plucked Griffin's nametag from the table and fastened it to Griffin's shirt. "She's my partner. See you later, Chelsea." She grabbed Griffin's hand and pulled her past the staring Chelsea into the banquet room.

People were already mingling, standing together in small groups. Songs from the 90s were blasting through the sound system a little too loudly for Griffin's sensitive hearing.

Griffin braced herself against the myriad of scents and sounds in the room. "Maybe coming here was a bad idea."

"Oh, no," Jorie said. "This reunion is giving me great ideas for my next book."

Griffin had to smile. "Has anyone ever told you that you've got a one-track mind?"

Jorie returned the grin. "Normally, you don't complain about my one-track mind."

"True. So, what kind of book are we talking about?"

Jorie's eyes twinkled. "A murder mystery. All these unresolved issues and old resentments..."

"So I'm guessing Chelsea," Griffin pointed back over her shoulder, "wasn't a friend of yours?"

"I didn't have a lot of friends in high school, and Chelsea certainly wasn't one of them," Jorie said. "She was the head cheerleader and prom queen."

"Was she the one who ridiculed you for writing the shape-shifter story?" Griffin asked, trying to rein in the predatory rumble in her voice.

Jorie shook her head. "No, that was—"

"Marjorie!" A blond woman waved enthusiastically, nearly spilling her drink on the tuxedoed man next to her. "Yoohoo! Over here."

Jorie groaned. "Her. Heather Dettman, Chelsea's best friend." She put on a smile that didn't look convincing. "Well, at least she remembered my name."

Griffin pierced the blonde with a narrow-eyed stare. "Want me to do something very unpleasant to her?"

"Like what?"

"Hmm, I was thinking of turning into a liger, biting off her head, and spitting it across the room, right into the punch bowl."

Jorie's tense face relaxed into a smile. "Well, at least that would prove that my writing isn't so childish after all."

Griffin took Jorie's hand and linked their fingers, not caring about the sidelong glances that earned them.

They made their way over to Heather and her companion, and Jorie stood stock-still as Heather gave her a hug that involved only a light touch to the shoulders and air kisses. "I'm sure you remember Thomas, our star quarterback. We're married now." Heather slipped her arm through his in a way that displayed her wedding ring. "And you?" Heather's gaze strayed to Griffin, dismissing her. "Single? Divorced? Or did you leave your husband at home with the kids?"

Great hunter, no wonder Jorie didn't want to go to the reunion.

"Actually," Jorie gave Heather a sugary-sweet smile and lifted Griffin's hand that was still linked with her own, "this is Griffin, my partner."

"Oh. Oooh." Heather tightened her grip on her husbands arm. "That explains a lot. So what have you been doing with yourself all these years?"

Griffin squeezed Jorie's hand. *I'd love to see her face if Jorie told her the truth... being hunted by shape-shifters and becoming their dream-seeing prophet.*

"I'm a writer," Jorie said.

"A best-selling writer," Griffin added. She couldn't help being proud of Jorie.

As if on cue, one of their classmates walked over. She fiddled with a book in her hands.

Griffin caught a glance of the cover. The eyes of her liger form stared back at her.

"J.W. Price—that's you, right?"

"Hi, Sandy." Jorie gave her classmate a smile that wasn't as fake as the one she had given Heather. "Yes, that's me."

"I knew it! I recognized your style from when we were working on the school newspaper together. Would you sign it for me?" Sandy held out the book.

"Sure."

Heather looked on with wide eyes as Jorie signed her latest novel.

When Jorie handed back the book and Sandy's pen, she met Heather's gaze and shrugged. "Guess all that childish scribbling I did back in high school finally paid off."

A triumphant purr burst from Griffin's chest, and she quickly turned it into a cough. "Pretty dry air in here. They set up a bar over there. Want me to get you something to drink?" she asked Jorie. *Maybe some champagne is in order.*

Jorie nodded. "That would be nice. Thanks."

Heather pulled on Jorie's sleeve. "Oh, did I

mention Thomas and I have kids? Do you want to see photos?" Without waiting for a reply, she whipped out her smartphone and flicked through images.

Oh, suddenly she wants to be friends. Griffin sent Jorie a sympathetic gaze. *I better bring her something strong.* Using her height and a predatory gaze to clear the way, she made her way over to the bar. The smell of vodka and tequila burned in her nose, so it took her a moment to identify another scent—one she hadn't expected to find at Jorie's reunion. *A Wrasa!*

She spun around, craning her neck.

In front of the buffet table stood a tall, red-haired woman, her plate piled high with food. Next to her, half a dozen people jostled each other to get to the stuffed shrimp, but no one encroached on the woman's personal space. Even humans with their blunted senses could recognize a predator—at least subconsciously.

As Griffin stepped away from the bar, the sting in her nose lessened and she caught a whiff of tiger musk.

Apparently, the woman caught Griffin's scent at the same time. She turned.

Their gazes met across the room, neither of them admitting defeat by looking away.

Griffin stalked closer.

Just as she reached the tiger-shifter, Jorie caught up with her. "Where's my drink? God, I really need it. Griffin? Hey, Griffin!" She followed Griffin's gaze and did a double take. Her scent evoked images of a ray of light breaking through the clouds. "Quinn? Is that you?"

Quinn? Like the tiger-shifter from Song of

Life? *Jorie named her main character after her?* Griffin let out a surprised snarl.

Quinn finally looked away from Griffin and turned toward Jorie. "Jorie Price," she whispered, awe written all over her face.

Was it just admiration for the dream seer, or did Quinn admire Jorie, the woman, too? Griffin wasn't sure. She stepped closer to Jorie so that their arms touched, marking Jorie with her scent. *Mine. Paws off.*

"Shannon Quinn," Jorie said, a big smile on her face.

"Just Quinn. I still prefer to go by my last name," the tiger-shifter said.

After hesitating for a moment, Jorie stepped forward and hugged the other woman.

The tiger-shifter stood frozen, and then a short purr rumbled up from her chest.

It stopped abruptly when Griffin growled. Instead of backing off, Quinn lifted her upper lip in a snarl.

Jorie let go of Quinn and looked back and forth between them. "What's going on? Do you two know each other?"

"I heard about her," Quinn said, "but I never met her."

Jorie frowned. "You heard about Griffin? How...?"

"She's one of us," Griffin said, her voice low.

"You mean...?" Jorie stared at Griffin, then at Quinn. Her eyes widened. "I named my tiger-shifter after you, and you're really...?"

Quinn's eyes widened. "You named a character in one of your books for me?" Her cheeks were tinged red.

Griffin didn't need her nose to detect that

Quinn was equally pleased and embarrassed to have inspired Jorie's main character.

"Yes, I did." Jorie rubbed her face. "Wow. I had no idea that you're..." She lowered her voice. "...a shape-shifter."

"Your subconscious obviously had," Quinn said.

A microphone screeched at the head of the room. "Folks, we've got a video slideshow, so you might want to find a table," Thomas said.

Lightly gripping Jorie's elbow, Griffin steered them toward one of the small, round tables near the exit.

To Griffin's annoyance, Quinn followed them and lengthened her stride to reach the table first. She set her plate on the table and pulled out a chair for Jorie.

Griffin nearly lunged across the table to throttle her. Anger pulsed through her, making her forearms itch. *Is she suicidal?* Quinn had to smell the mate scent, so she knew Jorie was involved with Griffin. Every Wrasa with an ounce of brain would have stayed away. Griffin hurled a subvocal growl that only another Wrasa could hear across the table.

Instead of jumping back in panic, Quinn calmly met her gaze. Her lips curled into an amused grin as she sat next to Jorie.

Griffin glowered at her. She sat on Jorie's other side and used her foot to drag Jorie's chair—with Jorie on it—closer. When their chairs rested side by side, she wrapped her arm around Jorie and leaned her cheek against Jorie's head.

Jorie glanced up, visibly surprised at the public display of affection, but then leaned against Griffin.

Sucking in a lungful of Jorie's soothing coconut-and-spring scent, Griffin finally calmed. She kept an eye on the cheeky tiger-shifter while she pretended to watch the video slideshow.

Images of teachers, cheerleaders with yellow pom-poms, and teenagers on school trips flashed across a large screen. All around Griffin, people reminisced about who had scored the most touchdowns, who had dated whom in high school, and who had changed most. The slideshow held a dozen pictures of Chelsea and Heather and the other jocks and cheerleaders, but none of Jorie so far.

Griffin suppressed a yawn. Her glance fell onto the honey-glazed ham on Quinn's plate. Instantly, her mouth watered and her mood improved. No better way to stave off boredom than eating her way through the buffet while the humans were distracted by their trip down memory lane. She put both hands on Jorie's shoulders while she stood, again marking Jorie with her scent, and sent Quinn a warning glare. "I'm going to hit the buffet. Be right back," she said to Jorie and hurried to the buffet.

While the slideshow starring the popular crowd played on, Jorie studied her former classmate. During their high school days, Quinn had been an outcast just like Jorie. With her athletic skills, which Jorie now realized came natural to her as a Wrasa, Quinn had been sought after by every coach, but she'd been kicked off the swim team and the softball team for rebelling against the coaches' rules.

Like most of her classmates, Quinn had changed. Gone was the lanky form of a teenager and the T-shirts with names of bands Jorie didn't recognize. Now her copper hair fell untamed onto a black leather jacket that stretched over a muscular body. She still looked like a rebel, and if Jorie's gaydar—the one that had been delivered with instructions in Japanese—was right, she was also a lesbian.

I wonder if she had any clue back in high school. I sure didn't.

After a few minutes, Jorie realized she was still staring. She cleared her throat. "I was hoping you'd come to the reunion, but I wasn't sure you'd show up."

"I didn't come because of them." Quinn waved her hand in a gesture that involved the rest of the room and lifted her upper lip as if barely stopping herself from snarling. She leaned toward Jorie and lowered her voice. "I came because of you. I wanted to see if my Jorie Price... I mean, if you are really the Jorie Price who turned out to be a dream seer."

Jorie sighed. "Yes, that's me. I always thought I'd go to my reunion boasting about literary awards and having a book on the New York Times Best Seller list, not about having precognitive dreams about weird shape-shifting creatures." She, too, kept her voice low so people at the surrounding tables couldn't overhear them.

"And I always thought by the time our fifteen-year reunion came around, my classmates would have stopped referring to me as weird," Quinn murmured, looking like a cat who'd had her tail stepped on. "At least the classmates that count."

Ouch. Genius choice of words, Ms. Professional Author. Jorie winced and massaged the bridge of her nose. "I'm sorry. I didn't mean it like that. It's just that I had my life turned upside down in the last few months, and I'm still adjusting to that. It's not all bad, though."

"Obviously not." Quinn flicked her gaze toward the buffet, where Griffin was sampling the food. "She's more than your bodyguard, right? Judging by your scent, she doesn't just guard your body; she also worships it. I didn't think that a human and a Wrasa could have mate scent, but you do."

Jorie ducked her head, hoping the dimmed light would hide her blush. "Um, yeah, I guess we do. So if you know about us, why did you pull out the chair for me? Encroaching on a liger's territory is not a clever thing to do."

"Where's the fun in doing the clever thing?" Quinn grinned crookedly. "Your mate is a Saru. She's got too much control to start a serious catfight with all the humans around, so it's fun to tease her a little."

Jorie half-turned to face Quinn more fully and stared right into her eyes. She had learned that most Wrasa took it as a challenge, so she was careful not to blink or look away. "Stop provoking Griffin," Jorie said, putting the authority of a dream seer into her voice. "Playing stupid games with other people is something they," she indicated their former classmates, "would have done. I expect better of you, Quinn."

Quinn lowered her gaze. "Guess you're as

protective of her as she is of you."

"She's my mate," Jorie said.

Not looking up, Quinn played with a leftover shrimp on her plate. "Griffin is one lucky cat."

Was regret resonating in her voice? Jorie wasn't sure. *Don't flatter yourself. She can't have been interested in the awkward teenager you were fifteen years ago.*

One second later, Quinn's bravado grin was back. "No more teasing. I'll find another woman to play with." She winked.

Jorie nodded. *So my gaydar was right for once.* "Thanks. So what have you been doing with yourself for the past fifteen years?"

Quinn's leather jacket creaked as she folded her arms across her chest and grinned. "Despite predictions to the contrary, I've managed to avoid prison."

"I never thought you'd end up in prison," Jorie said.

"Then you were the only one who believed in me." For a moment, pain flickered through Quinn's green eyes before her old confidence was back. "You'll never guess what I do for a living."

"Whitewater rafting guide?" Jorie said.

"Not quite."

Jorie thought for a few moments. "Stuntwoman?"

"Nope. Much tamer. I'm a pastry chef."

Jorie clutched the table with both hands to prevent herself from falling off her chair. She stared at Quinn. "Did you just say pastry chef?"

"I know, I know. People always expect something much more adventurous." Quinn shrugged, her cheeks tinged red as if she was embarrassed by her non-butch job. "Or they think it's not a good fit for a cat-shifter because we can't taste sweets. I'm probably the only cat-shifter in my line of work, but I really like it. It's fun to come up with something creative that requires a lot of patience to make. Plus I can work at night."

"No, it's not that. It's just..." Jorie took a deep breath. "The tiger-shifter in my novel—your namesake—is a pastry chef too."

Quinn sat completely still, a rare occurrence for her. "But how could you...?" She blinked. "You... you had a vision about me?"

"No. Well, I don't know. If I did, I can't remember it." Jorie leaned her elbows on the table and pressed her fingertips to her forehead. "I still don't understand fully how dream-seeing works. Maybe it's all just a weird coincidence."

"Maybe," Quinn said but didn't sound convinced. "So what else can you tell me about your main character? I hope she doesn't die?" She laughed, but a hint of fear showed in her eyes.

Jorie touched Quinn's forearm. "Don't worry. She gets her happy end."

Quinn scrunched up her nose. "Please don't tell me she ends up in the arms of a man."

"Oh, no. Her love interest, Samantha, is this really cute human woman who—"

"A human?"

Jorie rolled her eyes. "Yeah, yeah, I know, most of you Wrasa don't find humans attractive at all, but it's fiction, so bear with me."

"I didn't say that. Why do you think I joined the school newspaper our senior year?" Quinn flashed her a grin. "It sure wasn't because I was interested in journalism."

It took a few moments for the penny to drop. *Christ, I never realized.* Quinn had been one of a few classmates who was nice to Jorie in high school, but Jorie had been oblivious to any romantic interest Quinn might have had. "I'm sorry I—"

"Don't worry about it. I got over it," Quinn said with a self-deprecating grin. "Apparently, we weren't meant for each other. You've got Griffin, and if relationships between humans and Wrasa weren't still taboo, I'd be holding out for a cute woman named Samantha."

They looked at each other. Both smiled. Finally, Jorie nodded. "Speaking of my better half... I think I better go and drag Griffin away from the buffet before she eats everything. The hotel staff didn't plan for a Wrasa's appetite." She squeezed past Quinn and, careful not to block anyone's sight of the slideshow, walked along the wall toward the buffet.

Griffin was still enjoying the appetizers. With a big, happy grin on her face, she gobbled down stuffed mushrooms. Normally, she didn't like mushrooms all that much, but now she was purring while she chewed, and when she finished the last mushroom, she twirled like a cat chasing her own tail and then rubbed against the buffet table.

Jorie frowned. *What the hell...?*

Griffin's nostrils flared. She pulled back her upper lip and sucked in air through her mouth, acting as if she was breathing in a drug. Her head jerked up. When she saw Jorie, her eyes flashed. She ambled over and brushed her body along Jorie's. "Jorie." Her voice was a sexy purr, making Jorie's knees weaken.

"You didn't have that drink you promised me, did you?" Jorie asked. She knew Griffin wouldn't risk it since Wrasa couldn't digest alcohol.

Instead of answering, Griffin continued to rub against her.

Chelsea was looking over from the table next to the buffet, a disapproving frown on her face.

Jorie gave her a weak smile and tried to push Griffin away, but it was like attempting to move a mountain. "Griffin? Griffin, stop. What are you doing?"

Again, the only answer was a rumbling purr.

Quinn hurried over. "What's going on?"

Griffin wrapped both arms around Jorie, pulled her almost painfully close, and buried her face against Jorie's neck.

"I don't know," Jorie said from her liger cocoon. "She... uh..." Her voice trailed off as a hot tongue swiped along her neck, making her shiver. Griffin's breath bathed Jorie's wet neck as Griffin sniffed her. Goose bumps covered Jorie from head to toe. Now she had to clutch Griffin too to stay upright. "She's behaving like... uh..."

"Like a cat in heat—or a cat who got her paws on a little catnip," Quinn said, her voice low so no one else could hear her. "Is she using?"

"What? Oh, you mean...? No." Jorie shook her head as much as she could in Griffin's close embrace. "Catnip doesn't even have an effect on her."

Quinn lifted both brows. "Sure. Whatever you say." Then she sniffed the air. She blinked and looked dazed for a few moments before she blew out air through her nose as if wanting to get rid of a smell. "Ah. So that was the scent I caught earlier before your arrival lured me away from the buffet. Did Griffin by any chance eat one of the mushrooms?"

"One?" Jorie snorted. "She was gobbling them down as if there's no tomorrow. Weird. Normally, she doesn't even like mushrooms all that much."

"I bet she still doesn't. Ever see how cats react to olives?"

"Yes." Years ago, Jorie had accidentally spilled a bit of olive juice on the kitchen floor. Her cats had gone crazy, rolling all over the floor, sniffing, and meowing for half an hour. "You mean...?"

"Yeah. There were olives in the stuffed mushrooms. And now your better half is as high as a kite." Quinn grinned.

Griffin started chewing on Jorie's earlobe.

"Christ. Let's get her out of here before someone comes over to see what's going on with her." Jorie indicated for Quinn to grab one of Griffin's arms.

"I don't think that's a good idea," Quinn said.

Jorie sent her a pleading gaze. "I can't do this alone."

Quinn sighed and grabbed Griffin's shoulder to drag her toward the door.

Jerking around, Griffin let out a deafening roar.

The buzz of conversations and the clinking of glasses stopped as everyone in the room stared at her.

Jorie forced a smile. "Uh, sorry, folks. She

never could hold her liquor." She turned her head and whispered to Griffin, "Please, please, behave and let Quinn help."

Rubbing her face all over Jorie's hair, Griffin finally hung between them with her arms draped over their shoulders, and when Jorie moved toward the door, she followed. Step by step, they shuffled toward the exit.

"Are you staying with your parents?" Quinn asked.

"No." Jorie swallowed. That had been part of the reason why she was reluctant to return to her hometown. Too many memories. "My dad died and my mom moved to Florida three years ago."

"Oh. I'm so sorry."

"It's okay." Jorie lost her grip on Griffin's arm.

Griffin immediately took advantage and tried to strip off her shirt. Buttons flew everywhere. Griffin purred more loudly and pressed her half-naked chest against Jorie. Her free hand came up and clawed at Jorie's blouse.

"Oh, no, no, no." Jorie caught her hand and pulled it away. "The... the elevator." She nodded toward it with her head. "Let's get her upstairs to our room." She was breathing heavily, not only because of Griffin's weight partially resting on her, but also because Griffin was covering her sensitive neck with little nips, bites, and kisses.

One of their former classmates was blocking the way to the elevator. He hooked his thumbs into his belt and rocked on his boot heels as he regarded the three flushed women in a close embrace. "Ooh. Wow. The dream of many teenage nights. Need a fourth person?"

Griffin lifted her head, probably about to growl at the man.

Jorie quickly pulled Griffin's head back until Griffin's mouth was pressed against her neck. She was in no mood to deal with this jerk. "Sure," she said coolly. "Tell your wife she can join us."

The leer dropped off his face. He huffed and pushed past them, back into the banquet room.

Quinn almost let go of Griffin because she was laughing so hard. "Wow, you really changed. You used to be so shy."

Jorie freed one hand to press the elevator button. "Not much room for shyness when you're dealing with an amorous cat."

The elevator doors pinged open. Jorie dragged Griffin into the elevator.

When Quinn started to follow, Griffin roared again. Her nose wrinkled like that of a hissing liger.

"I think I better take the stairs," Quinn said. "Which floor are you on?"

"Fifth."

"Then I'll see you up there." Quinn reached out to pat Jorie's shoulder.

Griffin growled and lunged at Quinn.

At the last second, the elevator doors closed between them.

Jorie blew out a breath. She wagged her index finger at Griffin. "No more olives for you, Cat-anova."

Purring, Griffin rubbed against Jorie's finger. Within seconds, she went from aggressive predator to passionate lover. She pressed Jorie against the elevator wall and trailed a string of hot kisses along her neck, using her tongue, lips, and teeth to nibble and tease until Jorie's legs threatened to give out and she had to clutch Griffin closer to stay upright.

When Griffin sank onto her knees and pressed her lips to one of Jorie's bra-clad breasts, Jorie realized that Griffin had somehow managed to tear open her blouse without her noticing. She sucked in a lungful of air, hoping it would help clear her head. "Griffin, you're drunk. You don't know what you're doing. And we're in an elevator. We really shouldn't..."

Griffin slid her tongue down Jorie's belly and nipped the skin below her navel. She grasped Jorie's hips with both hands.

Jorie gasped.

The elevator doors pinged open.

Someone cleared her throat. "Looks like Griffin doesn't need any help after all," Quinn said.

Clasping her open blouse together with one hand, Jorie held on to Griffin with the other, preventing her from pouncing on Quinn.

Voices approached from the other end of the corridor.

"Shit. I'll distract them, but you better continue this inside your room." Quinn hurried down the corridor and called over her shoulder, "Maybe we can all have breakfast together tomorrow morning."

"Sure," Jorie called back. Using her body as a lure, she managed to get Griffin to follow her to their hotel room. She fumbled with the keycard while Griffin covered her neck and shoulders with nips and kisses. Together, they stumbled into the room, and Jorie kicked the door closed.

Growling passionately, Griffin directed her toward the bed.

As soon as Jorie crawled onto the bed, Griffin pounced and landed next to her.

The bed collapsed under her.

"Griffin!" Jorie rolled around. "Are you okay?"

Griffin didn't answer. Her big body had gone limp.

"Oh, God, no." Jorie shook her. "Griffin! Are you hurt?"

A loud snore erupted from Griffin's half-open mouth.

Jorie stopped her frantic shaking. "Great." She climbed off the collapsed bed, took off Griffin's shoes to make her more comfortable, and stumbled to the bathroom. She needed a cold shower.

Griffin clutched her hammering head and groaned. She opened her eyes to little slits and blinked against the hurtful sunlight. Except for her shoes, she was wearing yesterday's clothes— and her shirt was missing all its buttons. *Oh, Great Hunter. What happened?* She looked around and realized that she was lying on the bed in their hotel room. The hammering in her head was caused by Jorie's typing from the small desk against one wall. Now fully awake, she swung her legs out of bed. Her feet touched the floor much too soon. She frowned down at the ruins of the bed. *What the...?*

She searched her memory for what had happened but came up empty. The last thing she remembered was eating her way through the buffet at Jorie's reunion.

The typing stopped. Jorie stood and walked over.

When she came closer, Griffin realized that Jorie's neck looked as if it had been mauled by an animal. A large animal. *Uh-oh. What did I do?* "Um, good morning," she said and sniffed, trying to find out whether Jorie was angry with her.

"Morning." Jorie sat on the edge of the mattress and peered at Griffin. "How are you feeling?"

Her scent indicated honest concern, not even a hint of anger. Griffin relaxed. "Like a human the morning after prom night. What happened?"

"You got high," Jorie said.

"Whaaaat?" Griffin shook her head but stopped when the pounding behind her temples increased. "You know I don't drink, and I don't react to catnip. The only thing I react to is—"

"Olives. And you gobbled down about a pound of them."

"Oh, shit." Griffin covered her eyes with her hands and peeked through her fingers.

Jorie nodded. "You can say that again. Quinn and I had a hell of a time getting you to our room."

Quinn... At the mention of the tiger-shifter's name, Griffin's headache increased. She squeezed her eyes shut and sank back onto the bed.

A cool hand settled on her forehead, soothing away the pain. "You're not jealous, are you? There's nothing between Quinn and me."

Griffin opened one eye. "Maybe not from your

side. But Quinn clearly has a crush on you. Not that I can blame her."

Jorie sighed. "It doesn't matter what Quinn is or isn't feeling for me. There's only one cat-shifter that I have feelings for." She bent over Griffin and peered into her eyes from only inches away. "Even if that cat has a nasty biting habit." She rubbed her neck, which was covered with love bites.

"Sorry." Griffin pulled Jorie closer and tenderly kissed her neck. "I hope I didn't hurt you."

Jorie shook her head.

"What happened after we came up here?" Griffin asked, peering at the collapsed bed with some trepidation.

"You were in a bit of a hurry getting into bed," Jorie said. "And then you fell asleep."

Griffin groaned. "How can I make it up to you?"

"Well, you can be the one to explain this," Jorie pointed at the collapsed bed, "to the hotel staff. And I seem to remember something about a lasagna and a night of hot, wild—"

A passionate growl drowned out the rest of Jorie's sentence. Griffin covered her lips with her own and proceeded to show Jorie how sorry she was.

Griffin let the front door fall closed behind her and carried the grocery bags and their mail into the kitchen.

Agatha, Emmy, and Will appeared from various places inside the house and weaved around her legs while she put away the groceries.

"Don't think you can talk me into giving you little tidbits from the fridge again," Griffin said. She bent and rubbed Will's neck, then scratched Agatha and Emmy behind one ear. "Now hush. Go back to whatever you were doing before I came home."

Will, always the obedient gentleman, lolloped back to the living room while Agatha and Emmy kept hanging around, glancing up at her.

Ignoring them, Griffin took the pile of mail she had tossed onto the kitchen counter and sorted through it. Two bills, the newest edition of the writers' magazine Jorie subscribed to, and a postcard from Jorie's mother who was on a cruise. The last envelope was addressed to her. She opened it with a flick of her finger, pulled out the letter, and started to read.

Dear Griffin,

As you probably know, our fifteenth high school reunion is coming up. You and a guest are invited to join us on...

Griffin stopped reading. She crumpled up the letter and tossed the paper ball onto the floor. "Here, girls. Have fun." Grinning, she leaned against the kitchen counter and watched the cats chase their new toy all over the kitchen.

###

About Jae

Jae grew up amidst the vineyards of southern Germany. She spent her childhood with her nose buried in a book, earning her the nickname "professor." The writing bug bit her at the age of eleven. For the last six years, she has been writing mostly in English.

She works as a psychologist and likes to spend her time reading, playing board games with friends, spending time with her nieces and nephew, and watching way too many crime shows.

Connect with Jae online

Jae loves hearing from readers!
E-mail her at jae_s1978@yahoo.de
Visit her blog: jaefiction.wordpress.com
Visit her website: jae-fiction.com
Like her on Facebook: facebook.com/JaeAuthor
Follow her on Twitter @jaefiction

Excerpt from
Second Nature

by Jae

QUINN PROWLED THROUGH THE DARK *forest. She stayed in the shadows and slid from tree to tree, from shrub to shrub, avoiding patches of moonlight until she was far away from human campsites. She slipped her shirt over her head while she walked, impatient to get out of her clothes. Under a sprawling oak tree, she tossed the shirt to the ground. Her shoes and pants followed until cool air brushed against her bare skin.*

Dropping to her hands and knees, she connected with the damp earth. Heat rushed through her. She clenched her fists in an effort not to scratch her burning skin and felt lengthening fingernails bite into her palms. Her muscles rippled, and she gasped as pain shot through her.

Jorie Price's fingers flitted over the keyboard, keeping pace with her character's movement through the forest. When Quinn stopped and shape-shifted, Jorie paused with her fingers lingering over the laptop and reread what she had written—or rather rewritten. This was the third time she had changed the scene. She stared at the blinking cursor, then sighed and rubbed her burning eyes. Was the scene finally working?

Her heart said yes, but her head wasn't so sure. Why would evolution produce a skill that was painful and made the creature helpless for a few seconds?

She reached for the delete button.

No. Deleting the scene felt wrong. She pressed her fingertips against her temples. *But how on earth does a 140-pound woman turn into a 280-pound cat?* Jorie slid down on the couch until she lay on her back and stared at the ceiling, the laptop balanced on her stomach. Her eyelids felt as if they were lined with sandpaper, but she couldn't allow herself to rest. Not before she had figured this out.

"I could really use some help from a cat expert," she said to Agatha, who had curled up at the end of the worn, comfortable couch.

Agatha eyed the laptop as if that would make the hated machine disappear from the favored spot on Jorie's lap. When Jorie looked at her, the cat turned and licked her bushy tail.

"And you, Emmy?" Jorie's gaze wandered to the calico ambling toward the kitchen. "No words of advice for your favorite can opener?"

"Meow," the cat said but didn't elaborate. She walked on, looking over her shoulder as if to make sure that Jorie would follow her into the kitchen to feed her.

"Very helpful, thanks. And I just fed you half an hour ago, so that 'I'm starving' act is wasted on me." She forced her tired eyes to focus on the screen, but instead of the scene, images from her nightmares flashed through her mind. Shivering, she shook her head to get rid of the images. "I need a break." She saved what she had written so far and opened her e-mail program. Despite the gnawing feeling in her belly that told her she should be writing, she clicked on a new e-mail from her beta reader. Maybe Ally could help.

Hi, J.W.,
Still having problems with the story? Have you thought about putting it away for a while? I know it works for some authors. Maybe write a short story or get started on a new project. You could even start the research on a sequel to A Vampire's Heart. I know your readers would love that.
Let me know what you decide.
Ally

Jorie shook her pounding head. Maybe putting the story away for a while worked for other writers. But not for her. Not with this book. For reasons she couldn't fully explain to herself—and certainly not to Ally, she needed to get this novel written. Now.

She dashed off a quick answer to Ally and then reopened her manuscript file. "No admitting defeat."

Her cell phone rang before she had written a single word, shattering the silence in the living room.

Jorie groaned. She set the laptop on the coffee table and got up from the couch before

Agatha could settle down on her lap. Barefoot, she padded into the bedroom, where her cell phone was charging.

"Hi, Mom," she said. Looking at the display wasn't necessary. Only her mother and her agent had her cell phone number, and since Peter had dropped her when she had refused to give up on her new novel, that left one option.

"Jorie, how are you, darling?" Her mother's warm voice came through the receiver.

I have a headache as if I'm about to give birth to Athena; my nightmares haven't let me sleep through the night in weeks, and I have a serious case of writer's block. Aloud she said, "I'm fine, Mom."

"Are you getting enough sleep?" her mother asked.

"Yes, Mom," Jorie said. "Must be all that fresh air out here."

"Good. And have you met someone?"

Jorie sighed and looked out her bedroom window. Her neighbor was stacking wood in the back of his pickup truck, and the fall wind rustled through the white pines at the edge of her yard, but otherwise, nothing moved. Osgrove wasn't exactly a popular destination for most people her age, but coming here had felt right. "Please, stop trying to set me up, Mom. I'm not here to meet someone. I'm here to write."

"I know, but..."

"Stop worrying. I'm fine on my own," Jorie said. "Listen, I have to get back to my writing. I'll call you tomorrow, okay?" She wasn't in the mood to answer more of her mother's worried questions about the way she lived her life. Guilt scratched at the edge of her consciousness, but she pushed it away and ended the call.

Back in the living room, the screen saver had come on. A small, red cartoon cat was chasing a ball of wool all over the laptop's screen. "That's how I feel." Jorie lifted the notebook onto her lap. "Chasing the elusive ball of wool, but never quite catching it." She stroked her fingers over the touch pad and watched as the red kitten was replaced with the text of her story. "Don't think. Just write."

Her fingers found their places on the well-worn keyboard, and she started to write. If she could get this book out of her head and onto the page, maybe the nightmares would finally leave her alone.

Ally stared at the e-mail that might as well be J.W.'s death warrant. She reread it, halfway hoping the text had changed. Of course, it hadn't.

Thanks, Ally. I know you mean well, but I can't give up on this book. I hope you'll hang in there with me.
J.W.

Ally whirled her desk chair around and jumped up. *Dammit. You're not leaving me any choice.*

The walls of her apartment seemed to close in on her. Her skin itched with the urge to shift, to leave the apartment and everything in it behind, and to lose herself in the simpler existence of being a wolf. Things were so much easier when she was running with the pack. If she shifted,

111

she wouldn't just strip off her human skin but also the guilt and sorrow weighing her down. In animal form, things were clear and simple: her loyalty was to her pack, and she was doing what was necessary to ensure the survival of their species.

In human form, things were not so black-and-white.

With a sigh, she sank onto the desk chair. *Wishful thinking.* Running away wouldn't solve the problem. At some point, she would have to shift back, and the guilt would still be there, waiting.

She opened the prologue of J.W.'s work-in-progress. *This book is dangerous.* She had to warn the council before J.W. could publish it.

Ally picked up the phone and punched in her alpha's phone number. Her finger hovered over the last button before she pressed it. *I'm sorry, J.W.*

The revised edition of *Second Nature* is now available at many online bookstores as an e-book and paperback.

Other Books from Ylva Publishing

http://www.ylva-publishing.com

Second Nature
(revised edition)
Jae

ISBN: 978-3-95533-032-3
496 pages

Novelist Jorie Price doesn't believe in the existence of shape-shifting creatures or true love. She leads a solitary life, and the paranormal romances she writes are pure fiction for her.

Griffin Westmore knows better—at least about one of these two things. She doesn't believe in love either, but she's one of the not-so-fictional shape-shifters. She's also a Saru, an elite soldier with the mission to protect the shape-shifters' secret existence at any cost.

When Jorie gets too close to the truth in her latest shape-shifter romance, Griffin is sent to investigate—and if necessary to destroy the manuscript before it's published and to kill the writer.

Something in the Wine
Jae

ISBN: 978-3-95533-005-7
393 pages

All her life, Annie Prideaux has suffered through her brother's constant practical jokes only he thinks are funny. But Jake's last joke is one too many, she decides when he sets her up on a blind date with his friend Drew Corbin— neglecting to tell his straight sister one tiny detail: her date is not a man, but a lesbian.

Annie and Drew decide it's time to turn the tables on Jake by pretending to fall in love with each other.

At first glance, they have nothing in common. Disillusioned with love, Annie focuses on books, her cat, and her work as an accountant while Drew, more confident and outgoing, owns a dog and spends most of her time working in her beloved vineyard.

Only their common goal to take revenge on Jake unites them. But what starts as a table-turning game soon turns Annie's and Drew's lives upside down as the lines between pretending and reality begin to blur.

Something in the Wine is a story about love, friendship, and coming to terms with what it means to be yourself.

Backwards to Oregon

(revised and expanded edition)
Jae

ISBN: 978-3-95533-026-2
521 pages

"Luke" Hamilton has always been sure that she'd never marry. She accepted that she would spend her life alone when she chose to live her life disguised as a man.

After working in a brothel for three years, Nora Macauley has lost all illusions about love. She no longer hopes for a man who will sweep her off her feet and take her away to begin a new, respectable life.

But now they find themselves married and on the way to Oregon in a covered wagon, with two thousand miles ahead of them.

Hot Line
Alison Grey

ISBN: 978-3-95533-048-4
114 pages

Two women from different worlds. Linda, a successful psychologist, uses her work to distance herself from her own loneliness.

Christina works for a sex hotline to make ends meet.

Their worlds collide when Linda calls Christina's sex line. Christina quickly realizes Linda is not her usual customer. Instead of wanting phone sex, Linda makes an unexpected proposition. Does Christina dare accept the offer that will change both their lives?

L.A. Metro
(second edition)
RJ Nolan

ISBN: 978-3-95533-041-5
349 pages

Dr. Kimberly Donovan's life is in shambles. After her medical ethics are questioned, first her family, then her closeted lover, the Chief of the ER, betray her. Determined to make a fresh start, she flees to California and L.A. Metropolitan Hospital.

Dr. Jess McKenna, L.A. Metro's Chief of the ER, gives new meaning to the phrase emotionally guarded, but she has her reasons.

When Kim and Jess meet, the attraction is immediate. Emotions Jess has tried to repress for years surface. But her interest in Kim also stirs dark memories. They settle for friendship, determined not to repeat past mistakes, but secretly they both wish things could be different.

Will the demons from the past destroy their future before it can even get started? Or will L.A. Metro be a place to not only heal the sick, but to mend wounded hearts?

Manhattan Moon
Jae

ISBN: 978-3-95533-012-5 (epub)
978-3-95533-013-2 (mobi)
Length: 28,500 words (novella)

Nothing in Shelby Carson's life is ordinary. Not only is she an attending psychiatrist in a hectic ER, but she's also a Wrasa, a shape-shifter who leads a secret existence.

To make things even more complicated, she has feelings for Nyla Rozakis, a human nurse.

Even though the Wrasa forbid relationships with humans, Shelby is determined to pursue Nyla. Things seem pretty hopeless for them, but on Halloween, during a full moon, anything can happen...

Walking the Labyrinth
Lois Cloarec Hart

ISBN: 978-3-95533-052-1
285 pages

Is there life after loss? Lee Glenn, co-owner of a private security company, didn't think so. Crushed by grief after the death of her wife, she uncharacteristically retreats from life.

But love doesn't give up easily. After her friends and family stage a dramatic intervention, Lee rejoins the world of the living, resolved to regain some sense of normalcy but only half-believing that it's possible. Her old friend and business partner convinces her to take on what appears on the surface to be a minor personal protection detail.

The assignment takes her far from home, from the darkness of her loss to the dawning of a life reborn. Along the way, Lee encounters people unlike any she's ever met before: Wrong-Way Wally, a small-town oracle shunned by the locals for his off-putting speech and mannerisms; and Wally's best friend, Gaëlle, a woman who not only translates the oracle's uncanny predictions, but who also appears to have a deep personal connection to life beyond life. Lee is shocked to find herself fascinated by Gaëlle, despite dismissing the woman's exotic beliefs as "hooey."

But opening yourself to love also means opening yourself to the possibility of pain. Will Lee have the courage to follow that path, a path that once led to the greatest agony she'd ever experienced? Or will she run back to the cold comfort of a safer solitary life?

Coming from Ylva Publishing in fall and winter 2013

http://www.ylva-publishing.com

True Nature

Jae

When wolf-shifter Kelsey Yates discovers that fourteen-year-old shape-shifter Danny Harding is living with a human adoptive mother, she is sent on a secret mission to protect the pup and get him away from the human.

Successful CEO Rue Harding has no idea that the private teacher she hires for her deaf son isn't really there to teach him history and algebra—or that Danny and Kelsey are not what they seem to be.

But when Danny runs away from home and gets lost in New York City, Kelsey and Rue have to work together to find him before his first transformation sets in and reveals the shape-shifter's secret existence to the world.

Crossing Bridges

Emma Weimann

As a Guardian, Tallulah has devoted her life to protecting her hometown, Edinburgh, and its inhabitants, both living and dead, against ill-natured and dangerous supernatural beings.

When Erin, a human tourist, visits Edinburgh, she makes Tallulah more nervous than the poltergeist on Greyfriars Kirkyard—and not only because Erin seems to be the sidekick of a dark witch who has her own agenda.

While Tallulah works to thwart the dark witch's sinister plan for Edinburgh, she can't help wondering about the mysterious Erin. Is she friend or foe?

See Right Through Me

L.T. Smith

Trust, respect, and love. Three little words—
that's all. But these words are powerful, and if
we ignore any one of them, then three other little
words take their place: jealousy, insecurity,
and heartbreak.

Schoolteacher Gemma Hughes is an ordinary
woman living an ordinary life. Disorganized and
clumsy, she soon finds herself in the capable
hands of the beautiful Dr. Maria Moran.
Everything goes wonderfully until Gemma
starts doubting Maria's intentions and begins
listening to the wrong people.

But has Maria something to hide, or is it a
case of swapping trust for insecurity, respect
for jealousy and finishing with a world of
heartbreak and deceit? Can Gemma stop her
actions before it's too late? Or will she ruin the
best thing to happen in her life?

Given her track record, anything is possible...

Charity

Paulette Callen

The friendship between Lena Kaiser, a sodbuster's daughter, and Gustie Roemer, an educated Easterner, is unlikely in any other circumstance but post-frontier Charity, South Dakota. Gustie is considered an outsider, and Lena is too proud to share her problems (which include a hard-drinking husband) with anyone else.

On the nearby Sioux reservation, Gustie also finds love and family with two Dakotah women: Dorcas Many Roads, an old medicine woman, and her adopted granddaughter, Jordis, who bears the scars of the white man's education.

When Lena's husband is arrested for murdering his father and the secrets of Gustie's past follow her to Charity, Lena, Gustie, and Jordis stand together. As buried horrors are unearthed and present tragedies unfold, they discover the strength and beauty of love and friendship that blossom like wild flowers in the tough prairie soil.

Broken Faith

Lois Cloarec Hart

Emotional wounds aren't always apparent, and those that haunt Marika and Rhiannon are deep and lasting.

On the surface, Marika appears to be a wealthy, successful lawyer, while Rhiannon is a reclusive, maladjusted loner. But Marika, in her own way, is as damaged as the younger Rhiannon. When circumstances throw them together one summer, they begin to reach out, each finding unexpected strengths in the other.

However, even as inner demons are gradually vanquished and old hurts begin to heal, evil in human form reappears. The cruelly enigmatic Cass has used and controlled Marika in the past, and she aims to do so again.

Can Marika find it within herself to break free? Can she save her young friend from Cass' malevolent web? With the support of remarkable friends, the pair fights to break free—of their crippling pasts and the woman who will own them or kill them.

Kicker's Journey

Lois Cloarec Hart

In 1899 two women from very different backgrounds are about to embark on a journey together—one that will take them from the Old World to the New, from the 19th century into the 20th, and from the comfort and familiarity of England to the rigours of Western Canada, where challenges await at every turn.

The journey begins simply for Kicker Stuart when she leaves her home village to take employment as hostler and farrier at Grindleshire Academy for Young Ladies. But when Kicker falls in love with a teacher, Madelyn Bristow, it radically alters the course of her tranquil life.

Together, the lovers flee the brutality of Madelyn's father and the prejudices of upper crust England in search of freedom to live, and love, as they choose. A journey as much of the heart and soul as of the body, it will find the lovers struggling against the expectations of gender, the oppression of class, and even, at times, each other.

What they find at the end of their journey is not a new Eden, but a land of hope and opportunity that offers them the chance to live out their most cherished dream—a life together.

CPSIA information can be obtained at www.ICGtesting.com
Printed in the USA
LVOW13s0946171113

361633LV00001B/3/P